MAGNOLIA AT MIDNIGHT

THE RED STILETTO BOOK CLUB SERIES

ANNE-MARIE MEYER

Copyright © 2021 by Anne-Marie Meyer

All rights reserved.

No part of this book may be reproduced in any form or by any electronic or mechanical means, including information storage and retrieval systems, without written permission from the author, except for the use of brief quotations in a book review.

❦ Created with Vellum

For my friends

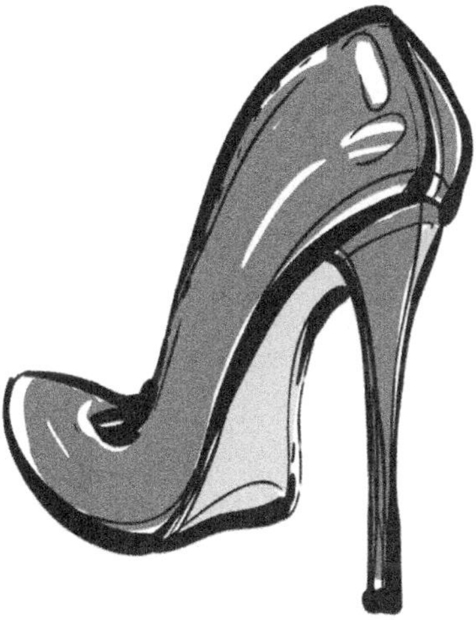

1

VICTORIA

And just like that, my entire life had changed.

I'd thought it would be easy to watch Peter take over the role of mayor. And in the beginning, I discovered that my inner will was stronger than I'd thought. Despite the fact that I hated the guy, I'd found it in myself to grin and bear the meetings I had to attend with him, but this was too much.

Standing in front of my mirror, staring at the dark navy satin dress and my red hair pulled back into a low bun at the nape of my neck, I glared at my reflection. Why did I have to go to his inauguration? After all, it was fairly clear that the town no longer needed me. Why debase myself by walking out onto the stage and clapping as he was handed the job that I had worked all of my life to obtain?

I knew it made me sound like a petulant teenager, but there was a part of me that wanted to scream to the world, "This is just not fair!" And perhaps, if I didn't constantly feel the judgement of my mother, I just might do exactly that. Whatever strides we'd made in our relationship after election day were quickly wiped away. We were back to the status quo.

I blew out my breath and dropped my gaze as I turned to walk over to my bed. The spinach and cranberry salad I ate for lunch sat like a rock in my stomach. That thought was strange to me—after all, spinach contained more water than anything else—regardless, that was how I felt.

"I'm losing my mind," I whispered to myself as I attempted to make my slightly too big wallet fit into the black velvet clutch Mom had given me when she walked by my room earlier today. She'd shoved it into my hand saying, "Losers support the winners even if we don't like it."

I took that to mean she could sense my desire to sprint from the house, skip town, and start a new life under a new name so no one would know my shame. And this was her passive-aggressive way of telling me to stop entertaining it.

Truth was, she wasn't wrong. I did want to leave this place. Start over fresh without the weight of her and Dad on my back.

But I knew I would only get so far. Dad had friends in just about every one of the fifty states, and camping in the woods and using leaves for toilet paper was not something Victoria Holt was built to do.

I liked my luxuries, plain and simple. And I didn't feel like it made me a bad person to acknowledge that. A woman had limits, and roughing it was definitely mine.

There was a soft knock on the door. "Come in," I called out as I grabbed my black, shimmery wrap.

The door swung open and banged against the wall. Danny stood in the doorframe with a giant grin on his face. He was holding a string in one hand that led up past the doorframe and a giant bouquet of roses in the other.

I narrowed my eyes as I stared at him. He and Shari had been inseparable since they came out as a couple. It was rare for me to see him without her pressed against his hip. There were a few times I had to bite back a snarky comment about how Shari was acting like a teenager even though she was older than him. I knew it was wrong to say, even if I felt it was factual. But my brother and my friend were happy together, so I was finding a way to deal with that internally.

Policing my comments, first around Peter and now Danny—I was growing as a human being.

I was just going to ignore the fact that I felt like Dante's Peak with all of this internal suppression. I was ready to blow.

"What do you want?" I asked as I shook out my shawl and then draped it over my shoulders. I knotted it in front of me, so I wouldn't have to hold it there the entire time.

Danny took that as an invitation to come in. Just as he cleared the doorframe, balloons filled my room and bounced off the ceiling. I stared at him and then up to the balloons and scoffed. He'd added *loser* underneath the word, *Congratulations*. Typical Danny.

"Wow, thanks," I said with a snarky tone to which I added a pointed look.

Danny chuckled as he walked over to my dresser and set the roses down. The balloons bounced as the weight that was tied to the end of the strings landed on the floor. "Hey, I had to wrestle these away from Bella. That girl's got some strength. She was ready to kill me when she saw me carrying them." He turned and gave me a wide smile.

That smile meant he was going to hug me if I didn't move fast enough. But the thought didn't register in time, and Danny was already across the room and wrapping me up in one of his famous hugs that ended with him lifting me off the ground.

"Danny," I squealed. As much as I hated how rumpled my clothes would be after this exchange, I was secretly enjoying it. He was the only family member who understood me, and once he and Shari became more serious, I was going to be left alone once more. I might as well enjoy this while I had it.

He set me down and stepped back. "Have no fear, your superhero brother is here." He pushed his hand through his floppy brown hair and grinned at me. "Plus Shari, too. We're all going to support you."

Tears pricked my eyes, and I turned so that he wouldn't see my reaction. Mom's words, replayed in my mind, were such a contrast to his, but I made an effort to push them out. It felt nice, knowing that there were going to be people there for me and not just for Peter. After all, I'd sacrificed. I'd given myself to this town. My happiness revolved around my success as a mayor. Without that, I didn't know who I was.

"Thanks, Dan," I mumbled as I grabbed my clutch and turned to face him.

His look of concern made my stomach flip-flop. He knew that I was struggling more than I was showing. Blast my inability to hide my feelings from him. But there was no way I wanted to get into this now. We could have this conversation over a few beers when I wasn't worried about smearing my makeup.

Raccoon eyes really didn't say *graceful loser,* and there was no way I wanted Peter to know that this election had broken me. I wanted to remain strong for as long as I could. Crying was for the shower, and that was it.

Danny paused but then nodded. Thank goodness he wasn't going to push me further. Instead, he linked his arm through mine and led me from the room. He patted my hand a few times as he escorted me down the stairs and into the foyer, where Shari stood talking to Mom.

When Shari saw us, her expression turned desperate as she hurried over. "Hey," she breathed out. From her red cheeks and frantic eyes, I could tell that her conversation with Mom had been a strained one.

To say my parents weren't happy that Danny had chosen to date an older divorcée was an understatement. I could only imagine the subtle—or not so subtle—hints that Mom was dropping Shari's way.

If I wasn't dealing with an existential crisis myself, I might have felt some pity for Shari. But at the end of the day, she got to escape to her house with Danny, and I was pretty sure that made up for any unpleasantries she experienced here.

I was stuck in this house. So in this crappy situation, I had it worse.

Thankfully, Mom and Dad were determined to be punctual, so all chitchat was cut short, and we were ushered from the house.

The ceremony was okay. Peter was too flashy for my taste. The mess of balloons and floral arrangements that adorned the flower garden behind City Hall was a bit much. But that was Peter, and everyone in attendance seemed agog at the sight.

After he was sworn in and dinner had been served, the tables and chairs were removed to create a dance floor. The DJ was blasting music, which was doing nothing for my headache. I wanted to leave, but every time I stepped up to tell Mom, she waved me away, telling me to mingle, and then walked away to fake smile at someone else.

It was as if everything I did trapped me. Be the mayor—trapped. Lose reelection—trapped.

I was suffocating, and all I wanted to do was push myself to the surface to breathe. But no matter how hard I tried, I couldn't quite get there.

Sighing, I headed over to the bar. If I was going to be here, I might as well drink. Besides, it was an open bar. If Peter was paying, I was going to take full advantage.

I nodded at a few twenty-year-olds who were hanging out at the makeshift tiki hut. The grass skirt that surrounded the bar was a bit too much, but Peter was a bit much, so it fit him perfectly.

The girls nodded back but then tightened their circle. I sighed. There was no way I wanted to join their conversation. I was just trying to be nice. Maybe that was the problem with my reelection—everyone in this town annoyed me.

"Rough night?" A deep voice drew my attention, and suddenly, I was staring into a pair of very familiar blue eyes. The bartender, who was also the chef at Magnolia Inn, grinned back at me as he moved to pour a glass of beer.

Seeing him here startled me. My tongue felt heavy in my mouth as I stared at him. I knew I was supposed to say something—after all, that's how a conversation worked—but I was exhausted and shocked, so words were a luxury I could not afford.

He raised his eyebrows as he finished filling the glass, and then he handed it over to a beefy man with a mustache who was waiting for it. The man slipped a dollar into the tip jar, and the blue-eyed bartender—whose name I had forgotten—thanked him before turning his attention back to me.

"Name's Brett. We met a while ago at the club across the bridge." He leaned closer. "I work with Maggie at the inn."

"I know," I blurted out. Geez, no words, and then suddenly I was literally yelling at the guy.

Thankfully, Brett didn't seem startled. Instead he just chuckled as he grabbed a bottle of wine from the fridge and began to fill the flute in front of him. "You doing okay?" he asked as he handed the full glass to Serenity, the woman who owned the grocery store in town. She gave him a smile followed by a wink before she turned away from the bar and disappeared back into the crowd.

I sighed as I shook my head and leaned against the bar for support. This entire evening had been a flop, and coming face-to-face with Brett was the icing on the cake.

Everyone in town now knew I was a loser, and they weren't shy about showing it. If another person gave me a sympathetic smile or nod, I was going to explode. "Can I get a beer?" I asked as I turned my attention back to Brett. He had been staring at me, and as soon as our gazes met, he straightened and cleared his throat.

His reaction was strange, and for a moment, I allowed myself to think that it might have meant something, but then I chased that idea out of my head. He was just marveling at my pathetic state, that was all. The once strong and confident Victoria had been knocked down. I was a museum exhibit now.

"Are you sure that's all you need?" Brett asked as he grabbed a glass and began to pour.

I narrowed my eyes. "What does that mean?"

Brett's eyes widened. "I wasn't—that wasn't—" He cleared his throat. "I was just joking." He finished filling the glass and then handed it over to me.

I took a drink. "Great. My life is a joke."

"I didn't mean that—"

I raised my hand, effectively stopping him. "It's fine. Laugh it up. I mean, I would too if I were witnessing this pathetic person in front of you." I waved my hand toward myself.

Brett's smile faltered for a moment as he stared at me. "Pathetic person?" His voice was soft, and I felt his confusion. It sent my heart racing in a way that I couldn't quite describe. It was both exciting and exhilarating.

Needing a break from the confusion that came from him, I sucked in my breath and turned toward the throng of people dancing. They were celebrating and happy. It was hard not to feel hurt. After all, they were celebrating my demise.

I sighed. I couldn't dwell on that.

Even though I didn't know where I was going with my life, I was kind of excited to leave the world of politics behind me. The constant pressure to do well—to perform well—was crushing. It might just have been the beer talking, but I slowly felt more relaxed the longer the evening dragged on. My connection to this world was fading, and I could feel its icy-cold fingers loosen their grip on my soul.

"You doing okay?" Maggie asked. She'd broken from the crowd and approached me. I could see the pity in her gaze, but I chose to ignore it. I was trying to let more people into my life, and all of the women in the book club had proven they would stick by me even when I was a curmudgeon. They'd earned my respect, which was the highest level of praise a person could expect from me.

I shrugged and nodded. "I'm getting there."

Maggie wrapped an arm around my shoulders and gave me a squeeze. "Well, we are all here to support you." She waved to Shari, Clementine, Archer, Jake, and Danny, who were all congregated at the edge of the dance floor.

I scoffed. "Not the new mayor?"

Maggie chuckled. "Nope. I'm lucky that I don't know of the legacy of Peter." She wrinkled her nose. "You'll always be the mayor who greeted me when I first came to Magnolia."

A pit formed in my stomach. Maggie was making me feel guilty for being so sour. She was nice, and out of everyone in town, she was the one that I felt got me. Or at least accepted me for where I was at.

"Thanks," I whispered.

"So what are you plans now that you are out of a job?" She dropped her arm and turned to grab some pretzels from the bar.

I sighed. "I'm not sure. I fear I've caused headaches for a lot of the residents. They might not be too happy with me coming around and begging for a job." I tucked a loose strand of hair behind my ear and blew out my breath.

Maggie was nodding and munching at the same time. "So you don't have a lot of options?" she asked. I watched her meet Brett's gaze. There was some kind of exchange between them, but I wasn't sure what it meant.

"Not really," I said slowly as I eyed the two of them.

"Perfect. It's settled, then," Maggie said as she pushed away from the bar. "You're coming to work at the inn."

I sputtered as I shook my head. There was no way I was going to ruin the only relationship I had that was somewhat decent by working for Maggie. It wouldn't be long before she learned about my annoying quirks and stubborn behavior. The last thing I needed was to alienate my friend and end up jobless *and* alone. I could only go so low.

Maggie patted my shoulder. "You'll learn I'm more resilient than I look. I'm sure we'll get along just fine." Her smile was carefree and relaxed. As if this was the only option that made sense for me.

As much as I wanted to say that she was just pitying me, she seemed genuinely excited. Did she really want me there?

"Plus, you'll be helping Brett and me out." Maggie knocked her fist down on the bar in Brett's direction.

He nodded and smiled as he dried a glass. "Agreed."

"Wait, what? You want me to work with Brett?" I shook my head. *That* was a big mistake. He was cute. He was sexy. And spending my days with him wouldn't end well. Not with my history with men.

"Nonsense. Brett's been complaining that he needs a hand in the kitchen to help with prep, and I need help turning around rooms. It'll be perfect." She smiled and then moved back toward the group she'd broken away from as if this conversation was over and she had won.

I watched her leave, stunned by what had happened. I blinked, the desire to hate her for putting me in this situation grew inside of me, but at the same time, my respect for her game was growing as well. Making a declaration and not waiting for a response was my move, and she'd executed it perfectly.

Blast that woman.

"I wouldn't fight it."

I turned to see Brett smiling at me. "Who says I'm fighting it?" I asked as I tucked my hair behind my ear. It had shaken loose with my forceful objection to Maggie's offer.

Brett narrowed his eyes as he set his hand down on the bar and leaned toward me. That movement brought him close, and suddenly, I felt shy. I wanted to retreat. How well could he see into my thoughts? What if he saw who I really was? What would he think? Would he run?

He would. I knew the answer to that question, which is why I felt like an idiot for thinking it.

All men ran when it came to Victoria Holt. Either I intimidated them or scared them. It was both a blessing and a curse.

"I can see it in your eyes." He held my gaze. This prolonged exchange made me feel exposed.

Could he really see how I felt? Did he know?

And then I felt like an even bigger idiot. Of course he couldn't see. Eyes didn't work like that. He could believe what he wanted, but the truth was, I wasn't scared. I was annoyed, and I was alone.

But I wasn't scared.

At least, that was what I was going to tell myself.

Even if it was a lie, it was the only way I was going to survive.

And right now that was all I could do.

Survive.

2

FIONA

"Slow night," Mom said as she moved toward the door of the coffee shop and flipped the open sign to closed. Then she set the lock, the click echoing in the empty dining room.

I sighed as I leaned my hip against the counter and folded my arms. My feet ached from standing in one spot. The burn on my finger throbbed—the out-of-control espresso machine had gotten cranky with me again. My entire body felt ancient as I rubbed the knot in my shoulder with my uninjured hand.

Blake was sitting in a far booth, his face illuminated by his tablet, which was on the table in front of him. I glanced at the clock and mentally scolded myself. It was nine thirty and my baby was still awake. I was becoming the type of mother I'd looked down on before I had a child of my own.

Oh, the things you learn when you are actually in a situation instead of an outsider looking in.

Mom made her way around the counter and pressed on the drawer release button for the register. It dinged and slid open. She pulled the bills from under the clamps and set them down on the counter next to her.

I busied myself with gathering the dishes and bringing them to the sink in the back to get washed. We had a good hour of cleanup before we could close the shop down fully and head upstairs. Which meant my son wasn't going to be in his bed at a decent time. Which meant he was going to be overtired and putting him down was going to be a battle.

A battle that I didn't have the strength nor the mental fortitude to handle.

"This is a disaster," I whispered to myself as I flipped on the faucet and watched the water cascade over the dishes while it warmed up.

Thankfully, there was something mind-numbing about washing dishes, and eventually, I lost myself in the movement. I was able to push out my worries and frustrations with myself and my current life status and, instead, tackle the dried-on fruit that coated the blenders. A bit of warm water and some elbow grease was all it took to get the plastic interiors sparkling again—if only that was all it took to get my personal life to find new life again.

It didn't take me long to finish up the dishes. After wiping down the stainless-steel counters, I moved back into the front of the shop and began cleaning the outside of the machines. Coffee had a way of spraying all over the place.

Mom had moved into the office to finish closing out the register and reconciling the credit card machine. I could no longer see Blake's head above the table, so I moved closer, only to discover that he'd fallen asleep at the booth.

Ugh. Now I was not only going to have to deal with an overly tired child, but I was going to have to wake him up, too. Yay, me.

Sighing, I turned off his tablet and wiped down the table. I made my way around the room, cleaning the tables as I went. By the time I was halfway through sweeping the floor, Mom emerged. The crease between her brows was more prominent than before. And for a moment, I saw a flash of concern fill her gaze.

I stepped closer to her, getting ready to ask her what was wrong, only to see her expression shift from worry to a forced smile. Was she hiding something from me? And, if that was the case, what was it?

"What else needs to be done?" she asked as she moved away from me.

I contemplated following after her but then decided against it. After all, Mom wasn't the type to express her true feelings. I knew that she wanted to appear strong and capable. She'd been that way when it had just been the two of us, and there was no reason for me to think she would change. After all, she'd convinced me to move back here after Dave cheated on me. I'd stupidly run after him to Tennessee when he convinced me that he was going to make it big in the music industry.

And moving from spare room to spare room of the friends he would pick up worked when it was just the two of us. But once I got pregnant with Blake, I wanted us to settle down. Buy a house and act like the quintessential family—but Dave had other ideas. Ones that didn't include Blake or me.

I thought I could change him. I really did. But that never works. And eventually I came to the realization that I needed to put my pride aside and accept Mom's invitation to live with her. I needed her help. And from the sound of her voice, she needed me near, so she could stop worrying.

What I had thought was a mutually beneficial move, was starting to look like it was stressing her out. But she would never admit it if I asked, so I just watched her mop the floor with a little more force than was necessary.

She was worried about something, but I knew she would never confess. Instead, I was going to have to live my life wondering what was wrong. Or if my being here was adding to her stress.

We finished cleaning the shop in record time. Thankfully, we were shutting off the lights and heading up the back stairs right at ten. Blake groaned when I picked him up, but he remained asleep. I cradled his head to keep it from flopping to the side as I waited for Mom to unlock the apartment door.

Once inside, I kicked off my shoes and padded over to the room that Blake and I shared. The upstairs apartment was small. A two-bedroom, one-bathroom place. We were cramped but somehow made it work. I was just glad Mom didn't object to Blake's toys that were scattered across the floor of every room.

If it bothered her, she hadn't made it known.

After changing Blake into his superhero pajamas, hastily brushing his teeth, and tucking him in, I stood in the doorway of our room for a moment. My gaze was focused on the lump that was my child. My heart swelled with both love for my child and regret. How could I have allowed myself to fail him like this?

I should have known that Dave was wrong for me. I should have walked away when I had the chance. I should have done so much more to guarantee that my son had the best life possible.

There were times, in my darker moments, that I wondered if I should have placed Blake for adoption. He could have gone to a home where he was loved by two parents. Where they could give him everything he wanted instead of living above a coffee shop while his mom tried to figure out what she was doing with her life.

I shook my head and grabbed the door handle, closing the door behind me. Once the latch engaged, I sighed, slumping against the door. I closed my eyes for a moment and chided myself for even entertaining my earlier thoughts.

I was the best thing for Blake because I loved him the most. I may not be perfect or make perfect choices, but I was dedicated to my son, and I would do everything I could to give him a good life.

I would live every day to deserve his love and affection.

"Tired?"

I glanced over to see Mom emerge from her room. Her makeup was off, and her greying hair was pulled up into a messy bun on top of her head. She had a thick creme mask on her face and was rubbing lotion on her hands.

I nodded as I massaged the muscles around my eyes. Every part of me was tense, and my eyes ached when I rubbed them. "Always."

Mom finished rubbing the lotion into her skin and then reached out and patted me on the shoulder. "I'll make us some tea."

I knew I should just brush my teeth and head to bed, but I was too wound up from stress. I knew that if I attempted to fall asleep now, my inevitable fate would be to toss and turn. If I was going to have any chance of sleeping, I needed to wind down from the chaos that I felt.

I followed after Mom as she headed into the kitchen. I plopped down on one of the kitchen chairs, resting my chin in my hand as I watched her fill the tea kettle and set it on a burner. The gas stove clicked, and a moment later, a flame ignited. Mom moved to take down two mugs and set them next to the stove.

"Sleepy time?" Mom asked over her shoulder as she stood in front of the cabinet.

I yawned and nodded. "Yes, please."

After setting the tea bags into the mugs, the string hanging down the side, Mom turned and pulled the container of cookies from the pantry and then sat down next to me. We munched on cookies until the kettle hissed. Mom stood, filled the mugs, and then returned to the table.

I held my mug between my hands, watching the steam rise and swirl. I took in a deep breath before I hastily sipped on the liquid. The heat burned my tongue and the roof of my mouth, but for some reason, I welcomed it.

It reminded me that I was alive. I felt like I was the walking dead most days.

"Careful," Mom said as she blew on her own tea. "You'll burn your taste buds if you aren't cautious."

I gave her an annoyed look as I pressed the top of my tongue to the roof of my mouth. She was right, and I hated that. "I'm not a child," I said.

Mom chuckled as she bit into a cookie. "I know. But you'll always be my baby girl."

There was an ache that rose up inside of me from her words. I knew she meant well, but there was a lot of unspoken history between us. I knew Mom loved me, but there was a hesitation inside of her. One that I couldn't quite understand. One that made me feel like a stranger at times.

"I know," I whispered as I took another sip of my tea. I wanted to speak more, but I wasn't sure what to say or how she would react. I figured distracting myself with the tea and cookies was probably a better use of my time anyway.

Whatever was going on between Mom and me wasn't going to be solved in one sitting where we were both exhausted from work. If we wanted to deal with the things that kept us from healing our past, we were going to need level heads and focused minds. Both of which were in short supply at the moment.

My stomach ached from the stress of the silence around us. Not wanting to slip up and say something that would only aggravate my situation further, I forced a yawn, stretching my arms out and leaning back on my chair. Then I stood, gathered up my dishes, and headed toward the sink. "I think I'm going to call it a night," I said as I threw away my tea bag and rinsed out my mug.

Mom didn't call me back to the table. Instead she brought her feet up onto my now vacant chair and leaned back. She brought her mug to her lips and sipped on the tea as if she didn't have a care in the world.

I hated being critical of my mom, but there was something about her relaxed state that made me anxious. Maybe it was because I knew our relationship was a ticking time bomb that was set to explode any moment now. She had things she wanted to say. I was certain she would deny that fact, but I could see the desire in her gaze. In the way she stared at me when we spoke.

The anticipation made me want to melt. I wanted to dissolve into a pile of nothingness. Waiting for the bomb that was this conversation—the uncovering of years of our relationship—exhausted me. I wish she would just tell me why she was disappointed in me. I wish she would let me in, because then I would know.

But Mom lived in a world where confrontation was just not her thing. She would rather remove herself from a situation than tell people what she really thought or what was really going on. Which I could understand if I had faith she would eventually let me in. But I didn't have that faith. Mom was going to be unhappy and stressed before she was going to talk to me.

And living with that hanging over my head was killing me. Slowly and painfully.

"Good night," I whispered as pain rose up in my chest. I nodded in her direction as I headed to the bathroom for a quick shower before bed.

"Night," Mom called after me.

I turned the shower on and stared at my reflection in the mirror as it was slowly overtaken by the steam filling the room. I wasn't sure who I saw staring back at me or how I'd gotten to this point in my life. How had I miscalculated so drastically? Why hadn't I course-corrected when I saw my life going down the crapper?

Why had I allowed Dave to sweet-talk me into leaving my family and following him?

If I'd known the pain that would come, I would have never done it. If I had known that my son would now be wrapped up in the consequences of my misjudgment, I would have walked away.

But I didn't, and now I was facing those consequences.

I knew the rules that came with making choices, and I knew that I had no one to blame but myself. I just wished I could see a light through the darkness that surrounded me. I needed there to be an end to this tunnel of my life.

I wished I could find a magical genie who would grant me three wishes. I would choose better for my son. I would do it all over again, this time changing my choices and deciding on new ones.

I would make sure my mother wasn't hurt and my son wouldn't have to go without because I had been selfish.

There was nothing I would wish for myself, only for my family.

Right now, they were the only people that mattered.

And they were the only ones who would matter in the future.

3

VICTORIA

I blew out my breath as I stared up at my ceiling. I rolled a chocolate caramel around on my tongue, reveling in the way the creamy treat felt on my tongue. So what if it was nine in the morning and I hadn't gotten out of bed yet? So what if I was watching chick flicks and eating candy for breakfast?

It wasn't like I had any place I needed to be. No one was depending on me. I was free…as free as a woman in her thirties living with her parents could be.

Thankfully, I overheard Mom and Dad talking about how they were going to be heading to their home in DC next weekend. That meant I only had seven more days of disappointed looks and passive-aggressive sighs to deal with.

I cheered internally as I flipped onto my stomach. Maybe with them gone, I would finally be able to think properly. I would be able to focus on the new Victoria—

whoever she was—and focus on building the rest of my life the way I wanted it to go.

It was strange and yet equally freeing at the same time.

A soft knock on my door caused me to look up. I moved to sit, but the knocker didn't wait for me to answer, and suddenly Mom was standing in my doorway with a disappointed look on her face. I instantly tucked the hair that had fallen from my bun back up into my scrunchie and wiped the sleep from my eyes.

That didn't change the way Mom looked at me. It was as if I'd broken her favorite china and she was never going to forgive me. Never mind the fact that I was the one hurt from losing the campaign. That was never going to matter. Mom was always the victim no matter what.

"Oh, Victoria." Her gaze swept the room.

The dress from yesterday was in a pile on the floor next to my shoes. I hadn't done laundry all week, and my basket was overflowing. I wanted to ask her to cut me some slack. I had just gone through an emotionally trying few weeks, but she wasn't going to care. Mrs. Holt didn't like excuses no matter how truthful they were.

I swung my legs off the bed and sat up. I rubbed my cheeks as if that was all it took to fix the mess that was my life. I knew it wouldn't change where I currently was, but if adding some color to my cheeks made me look less helpless, I was going to do it.

Mom's expression didn't falter as she walked further into my room. "You have chocolate on your face," she said as she tapped a spot on her chin.

I instantly rubbed the spot she'd indicated. When I pulled my fingers from my chin, I saw it was true, I had chocolate on my face. Ugh.

Mom's gaze finally fell on me. "Get showered and dressed and come downstairs. Your father and I want to speak with you."

Not sure what else to do, I gave a weak salute followed by a nod. "Okay," I mumbled.

Mom didn't say anything more as she turned on her heel and headed out. Once the door shut behind her, I let out a groan as I collapsed back on the bed. I closed my eyes and draped my arm over my mouth as I allowed myself to scream into it.

I was a failure. Pure and simple. My life was a mess—the state of my room was proof of that.

Not wanting to keep my parents waiting and further disappoint them, I sighed as I pulled myself off my bed and padded over to my bathroom. I showered quickly and dressed in a flowy black jumpsuit. After tying my hair into a bun at the nape of my neck, I settled on a grey wide-brim hat and grabbed my wedges and purse. I would need to decompress after a conversation with my parents, so there was no way I was going to stick around here afterward. I might as well be prepared to make a hasty exit.

Mom and Dad were sitting in silence when I walked into the kitchen. They both had a mug of coffee in front of them, and Dad was reading the newspaper while Mom scrolled on her phone. They looked bored and annoyed at the same time. A Holt family specialty.

I headed over to the coffee pot and filled a mug for myself. I was going to need all the help I could get to withstand this conversation. Once I had the mug clutched firmly between my hands, I turned to lean against the counter. I took a deep breath and offered my parents a smile. "So, what's up?" I asked and then winced. I sounded way too chipper. That was going to clue them in that I was uncomfortable.

Great.

Mom raised her eyebrows while Dad cleared his throat. His telltale sign that he was not happy. He shook the newspaper so he could refold it and set it down next to him. He turned and nodded toward the empty chair between them. "Sit."

Feeling like a kid again, all I could do was nod and head over to sit between my parents. I hated how I could go from a confident woman to a child with one look. My life was truly a mess.

I counted the seconds until someone spoke. It felt like an eternity before Dad took in a deep breath as if what he was about to say was going to take all of his energy.

"Your mother and I are selling this house."

I blinked. What? I turned to look at Mom and then back to Dad. "You're what?"

Dad's face turned sour. I could tell that he didn't like me questioning him. "We plan on spending more time in DC, so we will be making the house there our full-time home. This house was for you while you were mayor, but since you weren't reelected, it's time for you to move out and for us to move on."

Hot tears stung my eyes. They weren't about Dad selling this house or him telling me it was time to move out on my own—I was an adult and understood I couldn't live here forever. But it was the reason *why* he was doing this. It was because of my failure. The failure of my mayoral run. The failure to be who he wanted me to be.

Not wanting to show weakness in front of my parents, I cleared my throat and nodded. "Okay. How long do I have?"

Dad cleared his throat. "We want you out by the end of the week."

I stared at him. The weight of the world felt as if it were bearing down on me. I wasn't even going to have time to mourn the loss of my job. I was excepted to pick myself up and move forward as if nothing had happened. After all, that was what Holts did. Sympathy was a sign of weakness, and there was no way Dad wanted to appear weak.

Feeling as if the walls were closing in on me, I pushed my chair out and stood. There was a tightness in my throat, and I felt as if I couldn't breathe. I needed to get out of here and fast. "Okay, I'm gone. I'll leave right now," I whispered as I headed over to my purse and slipped it onto my shoulder.

"Victoria," Mom called after me, but I didn't stop to hear what she had to say.

If I didn't leave now, I was going to break. And there was no way I was going to give my family the satisfaction of seeing that.

"You're being overly dramatic."

I shut the door on Mom's words and hurried over to my car. Once I was out of the driveway and down the road, I let out the breath that I didn't realize I'd been holding. The red light that I stopped at blurred as tears filled my eyes. It was as if leaving had broken the dam that had helped me to keep my emotions at bay.

My life was in a plummet that I couldn't stop even if I tried.

I thought I was going to drive around Magnolia until I eventually got tired and pulled into a parking lot by the ocean to relax, but that didn't happen. Somehow, I'd made my way to the inn and found myself pulling into an empty parking spot. I threw my car into park and just stared at the building in front of me. It was morning, but I could make out the rooms that were awake for the day. Their drapes were open, and I could see light coming from inside.

The front door to the inn opened, and Maggie stepped out. She bent down and picked up the stack of newspapers sitting on the porch. I wondered if she'd sensed me staring at her because, a moment later, she straightened and swept her gaze around. It fell on me before I could duck, and suddenly she was staring straight at me.

Realizing that I was caught, I raised my hand from the steering wheel in a half wave. She frowned as she leaned forward, visibly squinting in my direction. It only took a moment for her to acknowledge me and wave back.

I don't know why I thought she would be satisfied with a wave, but I felt genuinely surprised when she set the newspapers on a nearby rocker and hurried down the stairs. I swallowed as I swiped at my eyes and straightened in my seat. Then I took a deep breath, pulled on my door handle, and stepped out onto the gravel.

I forced a smile as Maggie neared. She looked entirely too happy for this early in the morning—or, for that matter, to see me. It felt strange that my presence would bring someone that much happiness.

"Victoria, you came," she said as she walked right up and threw her arms around me.

Her hug pinned my arms to my side, and all I could do was awkwardly pat her back in return. She squeezed me tight and then pulled back, her eyes glistening and her smile radiating like it had earlier. "You're here to take me up on the job, aren't you." Her words should have been a question, but they sounded more like a statement.

"I, uh—"

"It is a huge stress reliever to see you. I'm booked solid, and I need all the help I can get. Brett was cussing in the kitchen this morning 'cause he was feeling the heat during breakfast prep." She blew out her breath, which shifted the strands of hair that had fallen across her face.

Now that she was closer to me, I could see the panic in her gaze and the dark circles under her eyes. She was frantic, and as much as I wanted to tell her that I wasn't here to accept the job, I decided to keep that quiet. After all, I could help her for today. If she needed me that bad, I could pitch in.

She linked arms with me and started to guide me

toward the front steps. Before I knew what was happening, I was inside of the inn. It was bustling. People were milling around the living room to the right or sitting in the chairs and reading books or chatting. On the left, people were sitting in the dining room, drinking coffee and munching on what looked like scones.

I knew Maggie was stressed out, but from what I could see, everyone looked relaxed.

"Are you sure—"

"The kitchen is this way." Maggie interrupted me as she guided me toward the swinging door on the far side of the dining room. She pushed open the door with one hand while holding me tightly to her hip with the other.

The sound of dishes clanking in the sink filled the air as we navigated around the large stainless-steel fridge. The kitchen was small but organized. My heart picked up speed when I saw Brett standing at the sink with a sprayer in hand, rinsing out a pot.

"Look who I found," Maggie sang out as she pulled me forward.

I stumbled for a moment. Brett glanced over his shoulder, and I swear his eyes lit up when he saw me. A smile played on his lips as he raked his gaze over me. Not sure what to do, I raised my hand halfway and gave a small wave.

"Well, look who the cat dragged in," he said as he flipped off the water, grabbed a nearby dish towel, and began to dry his hands. I tried not to notice how the muscles in his forearms flexed as he moved.

Who knew a movement so small could be so sexy?

My eyes widened from the thought, and fearing that I might actually say the words I was thinking, I cleared my throat and extended my hand. "Victoria Holt reporting for duty." My cheeks heated as my words met my ears. What was wrong with me? Was I trying to flirt?

Maybe.

I'd been so focused on my career that attracting members of the opposite sex hadn't really been on my to-do list. To say I was rusty was an understatement—but dating wasn't something I should be focused on. Not when keeping my head grounded and my thoughts straight was so important. I needed to focus on fixing my life, not making more drama.

Brett's gaze flicked down to my hand and then back up to me. His smile widened as he shook my hand up and down. "Brett Harvey. And you can just call me *Chef*." He gave my hand an extra squeeze before he dropped it and motioned toward the dishes that were stacked up next to the sink.

"Well, if the two of you are settled, I'm going to head out. The bedrooms aren't going to clean themselves," Maggie said over her shoulder as she pushed her way out into the dining room.

Now alone with Brett, my nerves heightened. He was so close and smiley. Why was he so smiley? Was he just naturally a happy guy, or was there something special about seeing me that had him grinning like that? Not sure what to do, I offered him a weak smile in return and then shrugged.

"So, what would you like me to do?" I asked.

Brett leaned forward. He was so close that his chest brushed my shoulder. My heart was pounding now. What was going on? Was he going to hug me? My arms twitched with the desire to hug him back—after all, his t-shirt was not doing a good job at hiding his chest, and there was a small part of me that wondered what it would feel like to hold him close.

Before I could lift my arms, Brett leaned back, holding up a dish towel. I stared at the dark-blue material and blinked once or twice before realization dawned. He wanted me to help with the dishes.

Duh.

He wasn't trying to hug me. I'd just met the guy, for Pete's sake. What was wrong with me?

Deciding not to delve down that rabbit hole, I took in a deep breath, put on my mayoral smile, and took the dish towel from him. "I'm a mean mincer. You know, for when I'm done being Cinderella," I said as I shook out the towel and then grabbed the pot that he'd just finished rinsing. I watched him from the corner of my eye as I dried the droplets on the outside of the pot.

"Really? I'll keep that in mind," he said as he slid on an oven mitt and opened the oven door. Steam filled the kitchen as he pulled out a sheet pan full of popping and sizzling bacon. My mouth watered at the smell.

It wasn't until just now that I realized I hadn't eaten anything for breakfast. Not wanting Brett to see me salivating over the bacon, I turned my attention to the sink and started washing a large platter.

"Hungry?" Brett's voice sounded close. I turned to see him standing behind me—inches behind me.

I focused on rinsing the dish. "Why would you say that?"

Brett chuckled. "I've been around enough hungry people to pick up on the signs." He leaned on the counter next to me, effectively entering my line of sight. His raised his hand as he pointed to my face. "Your eyes widened, and your lips twitched when you saw the bacon. You're famished." The smile that stretched across his lips caused me to focus on his mouth. His perfectly formed mouth.

For a moment, I wondered what it would be like to kiss him. Gosh, it'd been so long since I'd kissed anyone. I almost feared that I'd forgotten how to do it.

"What are you staring at?"

Brett's question snapped me back to earth. I blinked once, twice, until my brain fog cleared, and I could focus on what was going on in front of me.

"What?" I asked.

He chuckled. "You were staring at me." He reached his hand up to rub his mouth. "Do I have something on my face?"

I shook my head as I stared hard at the water that flowed from the faucet in front of me. I was fairly certain that my cheeks were burning. I'd been caught staring, and I wasn't sure how to handle that.

Since when had I become like this? I used to be strong. I used to be confident.

Now? I was a mess. A mess who stared at men and creeped them out.

"No. Not a thing," I finally managed to whisper. I turned to see Brett's soft smile as he studied me.

He raised an eyebrow. "You sure?"

I nodded—probably a bit too quickly—as I moved to again rinse the platter that I'd been cleaning over and over again. "Yep."

He paused as if he were waiting for something more before he drummed his hands on the counter and pushed back. "Alrighty, then. Finish those dishes, and I'll feed you."

I nodded as I picked up a mixing bowl and dunked it into the warm, sudsy water. I located the dishcloth and began cleaning. I could hear Brett moving around the kitchen behind me. I wanted to relax, I did, but there was no way I would be able to until Brett left the kitchen.

Even though I needed this job—and to possibly convince Maggie to let me stay at the inn until I found a place of my own—I couldn't help but wonder if, at some point, I was going to realize that coming here had been a mistake.

Being this close to a man who intrigued me this much was going to be a colossal misstep.

If I was struggling after being near him for less than ten minutes, what was I going to turn into while working next to him for hours every day?

A mess. That was what I was going to be.

So to save myself from inevitable insanity, I was going to need to raise my walls. I needed to guard my heart and mind for the foreseeable future.

That was the only way I was going to be able to last in this job that I so badly needed.

From now on, Brett wasn't going to be a sexy, mysterious guy. From now on, he was going to be Chef, and that was it.

4

FIONA

Mom wasn't in the apartment when I woke up the next morning. After throwing on my robe and slipping out of my room, I did a quick sweep of the living room and kitchen only to come up empty-handed. I was grateful that she was up and gone already. That meant I was going to be able to spend the morning getting ready with Blake without having to worry that I was somehow disappointing her.

I made my way back into my room to find a groggy toddler. He was sitting on his bed with his hair sticking up and puffy eyes. He rubbed them when he saw me, and as soon as he dropped his hands, his smile widened.

"Mommy."

I hurried over to him and pulled him into a hug. "Good morning, my love." I tried to flatten his hair that was standing up in the back, but it just sprang back up. "Did you sleep well?" I asked as I tightened my arms around him once more.

He let me hold him for the duration of two seconds before he pushed against me and wiggled. "Let me go."

I wanted to hold onto him forever—he was the only thing holding me to this earth—but I eventually released him. He crawled over to the other side of his bed and folded his arms, all the while giving me a stink face.

I stuck my tongue out at him and then brought my knees to my chest and hugged them. "We need to get ready, bud. Gran is waiting for us."

Blake folded his arms and shook his head. "I stay here." He then reached behind him to his dresser and pulled a few of his plastic dinosaurs off.

I sighed as I rubbed my temples. This was going to be a long morning. "Fine. You stay here while I go shower quick. Then when I get back, we'll eat breakfast." I slipped off his bed and stood. "Okay?"

Blake was already deep into pressing the buttons on the dinosaurs to make them roar. That sound only motivated me to get out of the room faster and into the steaming hot shower that was calling my name.

I showered in record time, even though I wanted to stand under the water longer. But leaving Blake alone for an extended amount of time was never good. Especially when he decides he's hungry and that he's old enough to make breakfast for himself.

I didn't have time to clean half a dozen eggs out of the carpet this morning.

Thankfully, once I was dried off and wrapped in my robe, I found Blake sitting on the floor of our room, flipping through a board book about dinosaurs. I gave him a quick smile as I dressed in a V-neck and a pair of skinny jeans. I blow-dried my hair in the bathroom, put on some basic makeup, and then headed back into our room.

After wrestling Blake from his pajamas and into a white shirt and overalls, I was sweating and hot. I blew out my breath as Blake wiggled from my hands and hurried from the room. I took a second to lie back on the floor and close my eyes, willing my body to cool. I hated feeling so sweaty after a shower.

A loud clang from the kitchen had me instantly standing. I hurried from the room. "Blakey, what are you doing?" I asked as I rounded the corner.

Bowls were scattered across the kitchen floor, and Blake stood in the center of them all. He was holding a small plastic one that Mom always gave him to use while she was cooking.

"'Ungry," he said as he moved to open the fridge.

I hurried to grab the egg carton from his hands and placed it on the counter. "I've got it, baby."

He let out a harrumph and then padded into the living room, where he grabbed the remote. Knowing that pressing the buttons to turn the TV on was going to distract him for at least a few seconds, I hurried to clean up the bowls, set the pan on the stove, and turn on the burner.

Blake let out a scream, signaling to me that his patience was gone and he wanted a show now. I knew I should feel guilty that he had as much screen time as he did, but I pushed that thought from my mind as I hurried into the living room. I was a desperate single mom, and I was trying to be more patient with myself.

"I know, I know. I took too long," I said as I pulled the remote from his hand and clicked on some cartoons.

He seemed to forget his frustration as he stilled. He was lying on his back with his ankle resting on the knee of the other leg. He was twitching his foot along with the intro song to some ridiculous kids show he was obsessed with.

I let my breath out as I hurried back into the kitchen and got started on breakfast. I needed to capitalize on the time that I had while he was distracted. While the eggs cooked along with the toast, I threw together some snacks for Blake in his lunch bag.

Tilly had agreed to watch him today since it was Saturday and she wasn't in school. That meant, along with working at The Hideout, I was also going to have to find time to run errands.

The show must have ended because, as soon as I plated our food, Blake wandered into the kitchen. I shot him a smile as I set his plate down on the table and then quickly joined him. I sat there, watching him eat as I pushed my food around on my plate. I wasn't really hungry. I hadn't been hungry these last couple of months since we'd come home.

I knew it was partially my fault. I was struggling with fully trusting Mom. It was hard accepting the fact that I had to come back. That things had gotten so bad in Tennessee that I needed to give up my freedom and live under my mother's roof once more.

Blake only took a few bites of his eggs before he slid down from his seat and made his way back into the living room. I contemplated calling him back, but then decided not to. A fit was going to ensue if I pushed him too hard, and honestly, I just didn't have it in me to argue today.

My phone chimed, so I picked it up only to find that Mom had texted me. I swiped my screen to read what she wrote.

Mom: Coming down soon? Business is starting to pick up.

I sighed, allowing my shoulders to slump before I texted a quick, "Yep."

I pressed the sleep button on my phone and set it face down on the table as I gathered our plates. I shoveled the eggs into my mouth, forcing myself to eat. I knew I was going to regret not eating later, so despite the fact that I didn't feel like it, I was going to eat now.

After dumping Blake's food into the garbage and loading the dishes, I brushed off my hands, gathered our bags, and then headed into the living room. Blake was hanging off the couch while watching his show. I found the remote and turned off the TV. Blake grunted with frustration, but he must have seen me put my shoes on because his tantrum subsided, and his focus was transferred to trying to slip his own shoes on.

As soon as we were ready, I pulled open the door and waited as Blake led the way.

Mom was right, the shop was bustling with people. They were either standing in line while waiting to order or standing off to the side staring at their phones while they waited for their drink. A few regulars were sitting at the tables, sipping their drinks, and talking.

"Good morning, you two," Tessa said as we walked by her. She adjusted her glasses on her nose and leaned forward. "How are you, little man?"

Blake moved to stand behind my leg as he peeked around me. Tessa's smile widened as she leaned in more.

"He's good," I finally said for him. I liked Tessa. She was sweet in a quirky, older aunt type of way. But her white hair and red lips were such a stark contrast that I feared she frightened Blake.

Tessa sat back as her gaze rose to meet mine. "That's good. And you?"

I shrugged. Any genuine answer would be a lot to unpack, so I figured the most basic of responses was best. "I'm good. You know, always busy. Always something to do." Blake took that moment to sneak his little hand into mine and pull me toward the glass cases by the register. I knew what he wanted, and I also knew that if I didn't give him a cookie, the entire shop—and effectively, half the town—would be privy to a good ole' Blake tantrum.

Why was being a mom so hard?

I gave Tessa a quick smile and then headed in the direction that Blake was pulling me. Just as we got to the cabinet, he pointed his chubby forefinger at the sugar cookies Mom had made yesterday. His grunt was synonymous with *I want that.* Not wanting to deal with a meltdown, I nodded and made my way around the corner and slid open the case door.

"It's eight thirty in the morning," Mom said as she moved behind me.

I stopped. My hand was suspended in the air, clutching the wax paper I'd just pulled from the box. I was crouched down, but I could tell that Mom was towering over me, and I didn't have to look over my shoulder to know that she was judging me. The way only my mother could judge me.

"I know, but I'm tired," I whispered under my breath. I wasn't sure if Mom heard me or not, but as soon as the words left my lips, I winced as I waited for her response. When she didn't answer right away, I looked over my shoulder to see that she'd moved away and was taking someone's order.

With her gone, I quickly grabbed a cookie, stood, and slid the door shut. Then I hurried Blake over to the only empty booth in the shop and settled him in with his tablet and the cookie. Tilly would be here any minute, and my stress level would significantly drop.

Then I could focus on working and avoiding Mom without the worry that Blake would interfere.

With Blake settled, I grabbed my apron from the hook behind the counter and slipped it around my waist. I'd just finished tying it when Mom walked over to me. "Ready?" she asked me, as she smiled at a customer that had just walked up.

"Yep," I said, but I knew that she wasn't listening to me.

"Hi, Betsy. The regular?" Mom asked as she stepped out of the way and motioned for me to approach the register.

"That would be great, Anna," Betsy said as she pulled her purse from her shoulder and rifled through it until she emerged with a handful of bills. I stared at her and then glanced over my shoulder to see that Mom had walked over to the espresso machine.

"How much is it, Fiona?" Betsy asked as she fanned out her money.

I blinked, knowing that I should automatically know what Betsy had ordered. After all, I'd been working here for the better part of a year. I should have it memorized, but for the life of me, I couldn't remember.

"What was your order? I'm sorry, I must have missed it."

Betsy's smile widened. "Oh, just the regular."

I rubbed my temples as the realization that this was not where I wanted to be washed over me. When I was a child, it was never my dream to guess coffee orders or spend the day making them. I'd been a free spirit. And now? I wasn't even sure who Fiona was anymore.

"I apologize, I have a slight migraine. Can you remind me of what your regular is?"

Betsy's eyebrows rose for a moment before she smiled and nodded. "Of course. Cappuccino with almond milk instead of regular."

I punched in her order and took her money. Then I handed her a receipt and told her to wait at the end. She gave me a sideways glance and then thanked me. Once she stepped away from the register, I sighed and leaned my hip against the counter. This day was already playing out to be yet another crappy one.

Ten minutes and a handful of orders later, Tilly came to pick up Blake. He complained for a moment until she promised to take him to the park, and suddenly he was ready to go. He grabbed his small backpack that I had stuffed full of snacks, gave me a quick kiss, and then grabbed a hold of Tilly's hand and led her from the shop.

I watched as they walked from the store and rounded the corner. Then I sighed. I didn't feel lighter with Blake gone. In fact, I felt heavier. The guilt was real. Someone else was spending time with my son. Someone else was being the mother I should be.

I knew it wasn't true, but I felt like the worst mom on the planet.

"Blake gone?" Mom asked as she emerged from the small office in the back. Her readers were perched on her nose, and the stress lines around her eyes were more pronounced than before.

I studied her for a moment before I realized that she'd asked me a question. So I nodded. "Yeah, they just left."

Mom glanced toward the large glass windows that lined the front of the store. "Oh, I didn't get to say goodbye."

I shrugged as I took an empty mug from a customer, filled it with coffee, and handed it back. "He was focused on the park that Tilly promised to take him to. I doubt anyone or anything could have distracted him."

Mom didn't move her gaze from the window. Instead she sighed and nodded. "Still, it would have been nice to see him off." Her voice grew quiet, which only affirmed what I was seeing. Mom was struggling with something, and she wasn't being upfront as to what that was.

I eyed her, wondering if I should ask. After all, if she wanted me to know, she would tell me, right?

As much as I wanted to say, yes, she would tell me, I wasn't sure. I wasn't sure about anything anymore. All I knew was I felt trapped. Being in Magnolia, although it was better for Blake, it didn't feel like home to me.

I wasn't sure who Fiona was, but I was fairly certain that the daughter who lives in her mother's small apartment and works in the downstairs coffee shop was not who I was. I wanted to fly, but I felt caged in a life that I didn't think could bring me happiness.

But I didn't know what the magic mixture was to bring me happiness. All I knew was that I needed to start looking, and I needed to start looking fast.

The rest of the day passed without too much self-reflection. Thankfully, the shop remained busy, which helped me keep my thoughts focused on mundane tasks instead of spiraling into the unknown corners of my mind.

Mom seemed happy with the distraction as well. She bustled around behind me, filling orders and handing them out. It was almost as if we were in sync for the first time in a long time. I even saw her smile once.

Around noon, Mom turned and nodded toward her office. "I can take over, so you can go on break. When you get back, I'll take my break."

My feet were aching, so I took her up on her offer. After

making a quick fruit smoothie and grabbing a croissant, I hurried into her office and shut the door. The noise from the front dulled to a hum, and I took in a deep breath as I reveled in the silence. I needed this break.

I collapsed in her office chair, setting my smoothie and food down on the only bare spot on her desk. I leaned back and closed my eyes, allowing my muscles to sink into the cushions that surrounded me.

Without opening my eyes, I gingerly felt around for my drink. The coolness of the plastic shot through me as I wrapped my fingers around the cup and brought the straw to my lips. The cool, tangy flavor coated my tongue and shocked my system as it went down.

I sighed as I opened my eyes and glanced around. Mom's office was tiny and cluttered, but there seemed to be a sort of unique system to how she did things. I didn't mean to pry—I knew Mom was private—but as I was sweeping my gaze over the papers, something caught my eye.

The words, *FINAL NOTICE*, caught my attention.

I blinked, wondering if I should look away but not being able to do it. The red words stared back at me like a train wreck happening before my eyes.

Mom was on final notice? From what? Why?

I reached down and picked up the paper, holding it in front of my eyes as if that would help me understand what they meant. My gaze skimmed the page as numbers began to register in my brain.

Six months past due. Twenty thousand dollars. Payment due by next month or you will be evicted.

I swallowed, but my spit was like glue to my throat. Mom was in trouble. This shop was in trouble. I was beginning to realize why Mom had been so short with me for so long. She was worried and stressed, and Blake and I being here wasn't helping.

"Are you almost ready to come back?" Mom's voice startled me.

I turned to her, my lips moving with the words I wanted to say, but I couldn't find the breath to say them. Mom's expression seemed curious at first until her gaze drifted down to the paper I clutched, and suddenly, her cheeks turned red and she hurried into the room.

"You weren't supposed to see that," she said as she pulled the notice from my hand and tucked it into a nearby drawer.

"Mom…what's going on?"

She turned to look at me. Her gaze shifted from me, then over to the wall, and then back to me. She twisted her hands inside of each other before she sighed and said, "We'll talk about this tonight. Right now, we have customers to serve."

5

VICTORIA

I grabbed the corner of the fitted sheet and tugged. Just as I pulled it over the mattress, the opposite corner popped off. I growled as I straightened. My muscles twinged, causing me to press my hand into my lower back.

Great.

Not only was I losing a battle with a fitted sheet, but I felt like I was rapidly aging while doing it. It was ridiculous, but it was as if this sheet was a strange representation of my current life.

Nothing was fitting, and nothing made sense.

"You're officially crazy," I mumbled under my breath as I tucked in the corner that I was currently working on and then moved around the bed to struggle with the corner that had just popped off.

"Talking to a bedsheet?" Brett's playful voice startled me,

causing me to pop up from where I was hunched over next to the bed. I scanned the room only to find him leaning against the doorframe with his arms folded and a playful smile on his lips.

Embarrassment coursed through me as I tucked loose strands of hair behind my ear and blew out my breath as if that was all it would take to cool my internal temperature. Not only was I warm because of my war with the bed, but seeing Brett standing there so casually made me feel flustered and out of sorts.

"I wouldn't have to talk to it if it did what I asked," I said as I motioned toward the bed.

Brett's gaze dropped down to the mattress and then back up to me. He winked as he pushed off the doorframe and crossed the room. He tucked his hand under the corner of the mattress and then nodded at me. "I've got this side; you tackle that one."

It took me a moment to comprehend what he was doing, but thankfully, my common sense took over, and I was able to focus on the task. We were going to make the bed together, that was all. He wasn't proclaiming his love for me or even making a move. If I didn't stop romanticizing everything he did, I was going to ruin everything for myself.

I was here to work and get my life figured out. That was all. Anything that impeded that was a distraction that I couldn't afford. At least, not until I knew the direction I was supposed to go in.

With the fitted sheet snuggly covering the mattress, I

stood and attempted to comb my unruly hair back with my fingertips. My hair was wavy, and when I was warm, or being attacked by humidity, my flyaways got a mind of their own.

"How's your first day going?" Brett didn't seem in a hurry to leave. In fact, he moved to the stack of bedding I had set on the dresser, pulled the flat sheet off the pile, and shook it out.

Not sure what he was doing, but grateful for his help, I moved to take the other side. We brought the open sheet to the bed, raised it up over the mattress, and let it float down.

"It's going okay," I offered. My voice was quiet and not like my normal response. I was losing my edge. I was losing my confidence. Eventually, I was going to wake up in the morning and look at myself in the mirror, and I wasn't going to recognize who was staring back at me.

If I wasn't go-getter Victoria, then who was I? How was I going to reconcile Victoria the inn worker with Victoria the high-powered politician who drank expensive wine and wore high heels for a living? My current tennis shoes and socks were a far cry from where I used to be.

Who I used to be.

"Wow, things are worse than I thought."

Brett's comment snapped me out of my reverie. I turned to look at him. "What?"

Brett tucked the end of the sheet under the mattress and then moved to the other side to do the same. "You. You're worse than I thought."

So I had heard him right. I scoffed and grabbed one of

the pillows on the ground and shook it from its case. "I'm worse than you thought?" I repeated, just to make sure he understood what he'd said to me and that I had heard him correctly.

But Brett didn't blink. Instead, he just nodded as he walked across the room to collect the folded-up comforter. "Yep. You are worse than I thought." Then he turned to me. "Have you ever had a mundane job?"

My body froze. My hands clutched the end of the pillow and my gaze focused on the tag the was stitched into the seam. It took me a moment, but I finally snapped out of my stupor to turn and face him. "What would you consider a mundane job?" Thankfully, I found my confidence and was able to project my question in a way that didn't reveal he was right—this was the first blue-collar job I'd ever had.

"Cleaning. Flipping burgers. Making coffee." He shrugged. "You know, the kind that you get from filling out an application instead of knowing the right people."

His words stung. Sure, Dad helped me get a job on an election team. He even pulled some strings to get me on the city council before I ran for mayor. But the way Brett said those words made it seem like I hadn't earned where I'd gotten. It was one thing to be elected. It was a whole other thing to work hard for the people you were sworn to serve.

My silence must have tipped him off to how I felt about what he said. Suddenly, he was standing next to me, holding out a pillowcase with a sheepish smile on his lips.

"I didn't mean that the way it came out," he said as he

shook out the pillowcase and then held it open in front of me. "I'm sure you worked hard for where you got."

Not wanting him to have the satisfaction of helping me, I grabbed the pillowcase from him, tucked the edge of the pillow under my chin, and shimmed the pillow into the case. After a few good shakes, the pillow slipped down, and I tossed it against the headboard.

"You talk as if you know me," I said as I moved onto the next pillow. "But you know nothing about me." I didn't mean for my voice to come out snippy, but it did. And for a moment, I thought about apologizing, but then decided against it. Brett was making some pretty heavy assumptions about me, and it was my job to stand up for myself.

Especially when my whole life and everything I knew about myself was changing. I could only handle so much failure, and right now, I was swimming in it.

Brett's chuckle drew my attention. My skin heated at his response. Was he laughing at me? Was my life that much of a joke for him?

"I think I've got this room handled," I said as I motioned toward the door. "I'm sure you need to get started on dinner." After I helped him finish breakfast and prep for lunch, Maggie had come in and snatched me away, declaring that she was behind on turning over rooms and she needed my help. I'd purposely avoided Brett up until this moment, but him being here in the room with me was making my resolve impossible to maintain.

How could I ignore a man who wasn't leaving my presence?

"Did I say something wrong?" Brett asked. He shifted his weight but didn't make a move to leave. Apparently, I wasn't threatening enough or something.

Not wanting him to know that he'd gotten to me, I put on an innocent smile and shook my head. "No. Nothing like that. I've just got things handled here. I didn't want you to get distracted and then struggle with dinner." The pillow I was working with slipped down into the new case, and I leaned over the bed to place it against the headboard.

"Are you sure?"

I nodded and straightened. "Oh, we're good."

Brett narrowed his eyes. "See, I hear the words that are coming out of your mouth, but the look in your eyes says something completely different."

I feigned shock. "It does? I'm not sure why."

Just then I saw Maggie walk past the door. Not wanting to speak to Brett anymore, I stepped forward and called out her name. A second later, she reappeared in the doorway.

"Did you want me?" she asked. Her hair was pulled back in a messy bun, and she was carrying a stack of folded towels.

"Yeah, I did." Then I glanced over at Brett. "Do you mind? I have something I need to talk to Maggie about."

Brett raised his hands. "No, I don't mind." Then he stepped up to Maggie. "How about I take these from you and get started on this bathroom." He sidestepped me and disappeared into the bathroom before I could protest.

I followed him with my gaze, even leaning forward to see if he was watching from the bathroom. The sound of the faucet turning on helped relax me as I moved to stand in front of Maggie. He could be here as long as he wasn't listening. I didn't want all of Magnolia to know that I was being kicked out of my parents' home. That I was officially a loser in every aspect of my life.

"Enjoying yourself?" Maggie asked. There was a subtle hint to her words that had me confused. As if there was a greater meaning to what she was saying instead of just the words that left her lips.

I eyed her for a moment before I pushed those thoughts from my mind in favor of focusing on why I'd called her in here. "I really appreciate the work today, and if you are willing, I'd like to take you up on the offer of the position." The words tasted sour in my mouth, but I was beginning to learn that beggars couldn't be choosers. If I wanted freedom from my family, I was going to have to take the first opportunity that was handed to me.

Maggie raised her eyebrows. "Wow, you sure?"

I nodded. "Yes."

"Well, I'm excited to have you on board. It's been such a relief to have you here." She reached out and squeezed my shoulder. "I'm glad you decided to settle here for a bit."

I smiled, grateful for her last comment. She realized that this wasn't where I was planning to grow roots, and that made this transitional process easier. "Yeah, I think it'll be good for me."

Maggie patted my shoulder a few times before she stepped back. "Was that all?"

I nodded, but then that nod slowly turned into a headshake. That wasn't all. I needed another favor. "My parents are selling their house in Magnolia." I blurted it out before I had time to police what I was going to say.

"Really? Why?"

I didn't want to get into the nuances of my family life, so instead, I just shrugged. "They want to get rid of some of their properties. Something about getting too old to handle so many." I gave her a sheepish smile despite the fact that I was leaving out crucial information. But she was my new boss, and admitting that my family didn't want to be around me anymore probably wasn't the best way to impress her.

"So..." Maggie raised her eyebrows as she studied me.

"So..." I took in a deep breath. How did I ask this without sounding like a total loser?

"You need a place to stay."

Her words startled me. I glanced up, expecting to see a sympathetic gaze shining back at me. Instead, all I saw was her smile. It was wide and inviting. As if this were the best news.

"How did you know?" I asked.

She reached out and patted my shoulder. "I know the look of desperation. I know what it's like to have nowhere else to go and to force yourself to ask for grace from someone." She leaned in to catch my gaze. "And I know what it's like when someone offers you that olive branch."

I blew out my breath as my shoulders sagged. I was grateful that she was so willing to help. And I was grateful that I didn't have to ask, but instead she just offered. However, her knowing that I needed help meant that I was doing a terrible job at hiding my pathetic life. If she saw it, who else did?

"You've got a room here as long as you need. It'll be small, though. Archer just finished adding a small addition to the back of the inn—we're trying out some new rooms for families to stay in. It's yours for the taking."

Tears brimmed my eyes, but I refused to let them fall. Instead I just smiled, and all I could muster was, "Thanks."

"Of course." She sighed. Then she clasped her hands in front of her and nodded toward the door. "Well, the inn's not going to run itself. There's always something to do."

"Yeah, of course. I'll finish up here and then come find you."

Maggie gave me another comforting smile as she passed by me. "That would be great. I'll have Archer get another key made for your room. You can move in tonight."

"You don't have to—"

"I insist. After all, that man has been sort of spacey lately. If I don't get him to do it now, he never will." She gave me a wink and then disappeared down the hallway.

I stared at the doorway after she left. My mind was overflowing with not only gratitude but fear that I was somehow going to ruin things with Maggie.

She was so giving, and right now, all I was doing was taking. I didn't like this imbalance. I didn't like owing anyone. It didn't sit well with me.

"Awesome."

I yelped and whipped around to see Brett standing right behind me. He was leaning forward with a goofy grin on his lips.

I glared at him and took a step back. "What's awesome?"

He paused before he straightened and glanced down at me. "I was in the bathroom, but I'm not deaf."

I swatted his shoulder, and the second my hand made contact, I cursed myself. What was I doing? Why did I keep flirting with this man? Not wanting to make the mistake of touching him again, I tucked my hands into the front pockets of my jumpsuit.

"What did you hear?"

He pulled back as he studied me. Then he shrugged. "Enough."

I glowered at him. "What is enough?"

He pushed his hands through his hair as he headed for the doorway. "By the way, I finished cleaning the bathroom. You should be good in this room as soon as you finish making the bed."

"Brett," I growled as I followed after him. "What did you hear?"

He gave me a grin as he stepped backwards into the hallway and then disappeared from sight.

"Brett!" I called again as I hurried to catch up with him. He was waiting just outside the door, leaning his back against the wall. I didn't realize that it was him until he stuck his foot out and nearly tripped me.

I caught my stumble at the same time his hand shot out

and wrapped around my arm. He pulled me closer to his chest, but not close enough to touch. My eyes widened as I slowly glanced up to see him staring down at me.

"Geez, I've never had a woman run after me before."

I glowered at him as I brought my hand up sharply, effectively breaking his hold on me. I raked my fingers through my hair, trying to tuck the loose strands back in with the others. "So you were listening."

He pushed off the wall, which caused him to tower over me. His gaze met mine as a wicked smile spread across his lips. "I already told you, I'm not deaf."

Great. He'd heard how far I'd fallen. He now knew that I wasn't Victoria Holt, the strong, capable woman. He was privy to my pathetic state, and from the way he was grinning, I feared what that meant for me.

He paused before he clicked his tongue and started down the hallway to the stairs. "I'm excited, though," he called over his shoulder.

I sighed. Fine, I'd play this game. "For what?"

He grinned as he held onto the banister. Then slowly, he wiggled his eyebrows. "I'm about to get to know you a whole lot better." With that, he jogged down the stairs and out of view.

"What does that mean?" I called after him. But he was already gone. Now alone, I pressed the bridge of my nose between my forefinger and thumb. I closed my eyes as the unease that I felt around Brett mixed with the butterflies that were flitting around my stomach.

As much as I wanted to say that I didn't care what he meant, that was a lie. I did want to know.

I wanted to know a whole lot about Brett.

And that sort of admission was scary.

Especially for me.

6

FIONA

Streaks of purple and orange filled the large glass windows as dusk settled on Magnolia. I closed the register with a slam and handed the change to the woman standing on the other side of the counter. She thanked me and moved down to wait for her order to be filled.

Thankfully, there was a lull in the crowd—no doubt most of Magnolia's residents were at home eating dinner. I was grateful for the quiet even though I'd been dreading it ever since I found Mom's eviction notice.

After she took it from me, she ordered me from her office and demanded that I not ask her about what was going on. She was handling things, and I was to mind my own business.

Her words hurt, but not more than the fact that she'd kept something so big from me. I wanted to ask her why she hadn't told me, why she'd insisted that Blake and I come home, and why she hadn't allowed me to help.

Not that I had anything I could help with. After all, I worked for her, and I was fairly certain that no one in Magnolia was looking to hire a single mom with a young child. Getting another job would mean finding childcare for Blake, and I wasn't sure if I was ready for that, much less if I could afford it.

Tilly was cheap because she was a teenager who watched him on the weekends. A full-time nanny or childcare center would take most of my paycheck.

Still, it would have been nice if Mom had been honest with me. Or felt as if she could depend on me. I couldn't help but feel that she still viewed me as a child. And that thought was most insulting of all. We'd been growing closer, in our own way. This revelation made the chasm between us feel even wider.

Mom smiled and handed the woman her Americano. They said goodbyes, and the woman left the shop, the bell tinkling as she pulled on the door. Now alone, the shop suddenly felt tiny and quiet.

I peeked over at Mom, who was staring out the window. I wondered for a moment if she was looking at the sunset or if she was purposefully avoiding my gaze. She knew as soon as she acknowledged me, I was going to have questions. And I could tell from her body language, she didn't want to give me answers.

"What time is Tilly bringing Blake back?" Mom asked without turning to look at me.

I leaned forward, resting my elbows on the counter and my chin in my palm. "She texted and said he was playing cars with her brother and that she could drop him by after dinner." I yawned and looked at the clock. Six thirty. "My guess is in the next half an hour."

Mom was quiet, and when I glanced over at her again, I could tell she had something on her mind. The weight of the world was on her shoulders.

"How long has it been this bad?" The question was out of my mouth before I could police it. Before I could come up with something more polite and less direct. Something that she wouldn't take offense over. I wanted to find a way to open a dialogue between us without her feeling attacked or as if she needed to play the situation down in an effort to protect me.

"Fiona, please." Mom closed her eyes, and her hands went to her temples. Something she always did when she was overwhelmed.

I studied her. I could tell that she was building a wall quickly. She wanted to block me out, and it was taking all of my strength not to take offense.

"I want to help," I said as I stepped forward with my hand extended.

Mom startled and glanced over her shoulder at me. Her gaze dipped down to my hand and then back up to me. "I've got this handled," she whispered. I could tell by the fire in her gaze that she wanted me to stop. That if I pushed her anymore, she was going to fight back.

"I'm here. In Magnolia. You wanted me to come with

Blake. If you can't trust me with this, why am I here?" My words felt as if they were choking me. I wanted her to be honest with me. Sure, as a teen, I was unruly and crazy. I ran off with a boy she hated right when Ted, my late stepfather, died. But I was a confused and broken kid.

I wanted to think that she didn't hold that against me, but from her actions these last few months, I was beginning to realize that I might be mistaken. Mom still kept me at a distance even if she had allowed me back into her home and back into her life.

"Fiona." Her voice came out as a whisper. I could see the battle going on inside of her, and I could hear her confusion.

"Mom, we have to start trusting each other eventually."

Mom pinched her lips together as tears filled her eyes. Just when I thought she might actually open up to me, the bell that hung from the door jingled as a group of teens walked into the shop. Mom brushed her cheeks with the tips of her fingers as she pushed past me and stepped up to the register.

I watched the window on our moment of vulnerability slam shut like a door caught in a heavy breeze. Mom was done with this conversation, and I feared that there was no pulling her back.

Feeling frustrated, I pulled out my phone. I needed to vent and get advice from the book club. They'd proven to be my friends, even if they were ten years older than me. We had things in common. Children. Frustrating families.

I had grown to trust them, and I needed their help now more than ever.

Clementine was the first to text back. She was ecstatic to hang out and offered to host at the dance studio. She said she had cheese and wine in her fridge that Jake kept consuming, and she'd rather see it in the stomachs of her girls than Jake's uncivilized palate. I responded with a quick thumbs-up.

Maggie was next to respond. She said that she would pass the information on to Victoria and that Clementine should instruct Jake to alert his sister. With the plans in place, I tucked my phone into my apron pocket and turned to focus on Mom. All I needed to do now was finish my shift, close the shop, and get Blake in bed. Then I'd head over to the dance studio and finally vent all of my pent-up frustration.

Thankfully, the evening progressed without any problems. Blake was exhausted when Tilly dropped him off, and the shop was slow enough that Mom let me sneak upstairs to put him down. After a quick bath and snuggle, Blake was snoring when I left him with the camera trained on him.

Tilly stuck around to help Mom man the counter while I was gone. When I got back down, she waved at me as she slipped outside. She was a great kid but looked tired. I ran after her to pay her, but she'd already gone home. I slipped the bills into my back pocket and made a mental note to track her down tomorrow.

After the dishes were done, the machines wiped down,

and the floor swept, I grabbed my purse from behind the counter as Mom moved to head up the stairs. She turned to look at me, her brow furrowed.

"Going somewhere?"

I nodded as I fished out my car keys. "I'm going to Clementine's if that's okay. We're having an impromptu book club meeting." I didn't want Mom to ask further questions, so I just smiled and pulled open the door. "Lock it behind me?" I paused and glanced back at Mom. "It's okay, right?"

Mom gave a soft *mm-hmm* as she made her way to the door. "I'm just going to take a bath and watch a chick flick. I'll probably be fast asleep by the time you get back."

I studied her for a moment, wondering if I should stay back. But Mom didn't look interested in talking to me, so I shrugged that thought off and gave her a wave.

The drive to the dance studio was quick. As soon as I pushed the car into park, I pulled the keys from the ignition and opened my door. Everyone was already inside. I kicked off my shoes to save Clementine's wood floors. The bottle of wine was already opened, and the cheese was out on a cutting board next to some crackers.

Maggie handed me a glass of wine, and I graciously took it. "Archer's hanging out with Jake if you need him to drive you home."

I raised my glass to that offer, clinking it against Maggie's. "He's a godsend."

Maggie giggled as she took a sip. "I would agree."

Clementine waved her hand between us as if that was

her attempt at stopping our conversation. Her nose wrinkled as she shook her head. "No talking like that around me. He's my brother."

"Tell me about it," Victoria said as she took a sip of her wine.

"Hey." Shari dropped her jaw. "Danny and I are discrete."

"Discrete like a bull in a china shop." Victoria slipped a slice of cheese into her mouth. She looked tired and worn and not her normal put together self. I made a mental note to inquire about her later.

"So, why are we here?" Clementine asked.

I set my glass down and sighed. After taking a moment to compose my thoughts, I turned to my newfound friends. "I need your help. Something's going on with my mom, and I can't figure out how to get her to open up to me about it."

Maggie tapped her chin. "Something?"

I nodded. "The shop..." I paused. I wasn't sure how much Mom wanted me to tell these ladies. I had a feeling if she was keeping it from me, she probably didn't want them to know.

But I couldn't keep this a secret. This was something that was too big to hold inside. It was going to take a miracle to save the shop, and a miracle wasn't something Mom or I could conjure up.

Maybe if we had more eyes on the problem, a solution could be found.

All four women were leaning in. Their focus was on me as they waited for me to finish my sentence. It was a little unnerving to have their undivided attention, but I pushed out the urge to shut down, and I spoke.

I told them about the letter. I told them about Mom's reaction. And I told them how I felt helpless. By the time I was finished, they were quiet as they leaned back. The silence that hung in the air was palpable.

"So?" I asked, glancing around at them. "What do I do?"

Clementine was the first to speak. "Honey, I don't know." She clicked her tongue. "Without more information from your mom, it sounds like there isn't a lot that you can do." She flicked her dark hair over her shoulder as she glanced around at the other women. "What do you guys think?"

"You're right; getting a job as a single mom is hard. Especially since there's no one to watch Blake." Shari tapped her chin. "Is Dave paying child support?"

My least favorite topic. One that made me squirm and want to sprint from the room. I knew the answer. After all, the proof was evident in the lack of funds in my bank account. But I knew why she was asking that question, and I wasn't sure if I was ready to answer.

I didn't want to open the can of worms that I'd worked so hard to keep closed.

I pinched my lips shut and shook my head. There was a collective groan as all four women pulled back and glanced between themselves.

"Fiona," Shari said, her voice both confused and forceful. I knew she was about to lay down some tough love, and I both loved that about her and feared it at the same time.

"I know," I whimpered as I covered my face with both hands. I knew I should fight harder to get Dave to pay. I knew that it was his job as the father of my son to help take care of Blake. But ever since I packed up Blake and took him to Magnolia, Dave had stayed away. I wasn't sure that I was ready to poke that snake den by demanding money.

What if he demanded time with Blake? Or worse, what if he fought to take my baby away from me? Was this a risk I was willing to take?

An arm wrapped around my shoulders, and suddenly, I was pulled in next to Maggie. She smiled down at me in a way that made me feel like things were going to be okay—even though I knew she had no way of guaranteeing that. She didn't know the risk I was about to take if I were to head down this road.

"We're here for you, Fiona. We'll help you come up with a solution," Maggie said.

I chewed on my bottom lip. Her words, mixed with the encouraging smiles from everyone standing around me, caused my emotions to heighten. I drank in the feeling of warmth and companionship that I'd grown accustomed to while in this book club and in our relationships as a whole.

We truly were a group of women who cared about each other. It was refreshing.

I took a long sip of wine before I spoke. I needed to clear my throat of the emotions that resided there. "Thanks, guys," I said, my voice coming out breathy.

They all nodded.

"Of course," Shari said as she reached out and patted my

shoulder. "I didn't mean to upset you by asking about Dave. I just know how important it is for you to be taken care of and how important it is for Dave to take care of his son. He should be paying child support, period."

I nodded. I knew her words came from a good place. And I knew she wanted to help even if what she said made me feel itchy. "I know," I said as I smiled up at her.

She looked relieved as she stepped back.

Silence fell around us. As if everyone was waiting for me to speak, to lead the conversation.

I cleared my throat, my questions resting there as I rubbed my temple. "If I wanted to pursue legal action against Dave, how would I do that?" My voice was barely a whisper—or at least that was how it sounded to me. I could literally hear the blood rushing through my ears as my anxiety soared.

Just saying the words out loud caused fear to build up inside of me. As if Dave had supersonic hearing and was going to show up at the door in a matter of minutes demanding that I hand Blake over to him. That I was somehow an unfit mother who couldn't take care of her son —which in this moment of my life, was kind of true.

Mix my personal issues with Mom's failing business, and Blake's stable life with functioning adults would be out the window. I doubted that many judges would take a look at my situation and award me custody of my child, much less full custody.

Everyone looked at Shari. Even though Maggie was also

a divorcée, Shari was the only one with kids, and she'd gone through the most recent divorce.

Shari placed her wineglass down on the counter and pulled her phone from her back pocket. She swiped on her screen. "I'm going to text you my lawyer's number. You need to start there. He'll give you a free hour of advice—he's my brother-in-law. He can give you some pointers on how to start."

My phone chimed, signaling that her text had come through.

"I'll let him know that you are going to contact him." She gave me a small smile. "Truth is, he'll probably tell you to first work something out with Dave. It's best to have the parties involved do their own arrangements. If that doesn't work, it'll move to mediation between lawyers." She patted my shoulder again. "Very rarely will it make it to a judge. So don't worry."

My stomach was in knots at her words, but I tried to push the fear from my mind and focus on her positive tone. It helped that everyone else in the room looked relaxed. It helped me to lessen my worry that I just might lose my son.

"Don't worry, Fiona. We're here for you. And in the meantime, we can brainstorm some ideas to help your mom." Clementine pulled open a drawer by the check-in counter and emerged with a pad of paper and a pen. "We can start by making a list of options and go from there."

I smiled and nodded. Even though I felt stressed and fearful, the fact that these women had my back made me feel stronger. Like I could take on anything that was going to come my way.

And from what I knew of Dave, things were about to get ugly. He wasn't the kind of guy who went down without a fight. And this time, I would be on the receiving end.

To say I was worried was an understatement.

I was terrified.

7

VICTORIA

I pulled into the inn's parking lot after our impromptu meeting with Fiona and turned off the engine of my car. I sat in silence for a moment before I took in a deep breath and closed my eyes. I tipped my head back and sighed.

The stress of the day surrounded me like a bad aura, and I wanted to dispel it as best I could. I wasn't one who normally believed in chakras or essential oils, but I needed all the help I could get to feel better about my life and the direction it was headed.

I'd stopped by Mom and Dad's house before heading to Clementine's studio, and thankfully they were out for the evening and hadn't decided to change the locks just yet. I was able to pack a suitcase for the next few days while I figured out my life here at the inn and what I was going to do with the rest of my stuff when the house was sold.

Panic rose up inside of me, so I took a few deep

cleansing breaths to calm myself. I could do this. I was capable. I could handle a lot more than my parents gave me credit for.

And I was going to prove that to them.

I shot Danny a quick text, telling him that we had to meet for lunch at the inn tomorrow afternoon. He responded with a thumbs-up. I tucked my phone back into my purse and pushed the strap up onto my shoulder.

With my suitcase in hand, I started toward the front door of the inn. This was my first official night on my own without my parents hanging over me, directing my every move.

Sure, I went to college, and I even lived by myself for a spell. But Mom and Dad had been everywhere. Always talking about my future in politics. Always dictating who I needed to dine with or get to know at the country club.

Now, things were different. I had no idea what they wanted from me. They had no say in who I was going to become or what career I would take on.

Just as I reached out to turn the handle on the door, it swung open. I startled, stepping back as my eyes focused on Brett. He was standing in the doorway, holding two mugs, and grinning like he'd just done something devious.

I furrowed my brow, attempting to ignore the fact that his presence caused my heart rate to increase and the butterflies in my stomach to take flight. It was just a ridiculous schoolgirl crush. An obsession because he'd been the first person to care about me since Mom and Dad kicked me out.

I didn't currently have real feelings for him, and I was determined to never have feelings for him in the future. An arduous task, but one I could accomplish if I put my mind to it.

"What are you doing here so late?" I asked as I heaved my suitcase over the threshold. Brett, thankfully, had enough sense to back up in order to give me some room.

"I wanted to be here to greet our guest," he said.

He handed me a mug and leaned forward to grab my suitcase handle. His fingers brushed mine, and tingles erupted across my skin. I snapped my hand back—a self-preservation measure—and Brett took full control of my suitcase. He gave me a smile and a wink as he began to drag it down the hallway to the left of the staircase.

I wanted to protest, but he looked determined. Even if I did say something, I doubted he would listen. The sweet smell of coffee and caramel wafted up to my nose, so I decided to focus on drinking whatever concoction he'd given me.

After a few sips, a sort of happy feeling washed over me. One that only came from a warm, sweet, and satisfying drink. I could feel my annoyance melt away as I followed after Brett.

The room he'd gone into was small. A twin bed was pressed against the far wall. A cheery, sunflower wallpaper adorned the walls—not my taste, but it would do for now. The room was simple, and I couldn't help but feel as if this was Maggie in room form.

Simple, sweet, and homey. She had a way of making you

feel comfortable in your own skin and yet desirous to do better.

Brett set my suitcase down on the floor and then turned. He eyed me for a moment before wandering over to the French doors that led out to the back of the inn. He leaned against the doorframe as if it were the most natural thing in the world.

I'm not going to lie. He looked good in my room. If Maggie wanted to stick a statue of him off to the side, I wouldn't complain. It would be a great thing to stare at while I went to bed and to greet when I woke up in the morning.

My cheeks warmed as I cleared my throat and moved to set my purse down on the nearby dresser. I felt like Ariel with the statue of Prince Eric. Man, I was a mess.

"Are you this attentive with all the guests?" I asked as I took another sip of my drink. Geez, this guy's cooking matched his looks. Sexy with a hint of down-home-ness—if there was such a term.

Brett glanced over at me and then shifted so he was leaning against the wall, his full focus on me. The way he studied me caused my insecurities to rise to the surface. I wanted to pull back into my cave for protection, but I also wanted to remain strong. There was no way I was going to let someone else enter my life and control me like my parents had.

I was bound and determined to find the new me—whoever she was. But there was something about Brett. Something in the way he stared at me. Watched me. It awoke a fire inside of me that I thought had burned out years ago. When I was with him, I wanted to be a woman. That was all.

I cleared my throat and, with it, all the thoughts from my mind. I raised my eyebrows as I stared at him, waiting for him to respond. We were in a battle over who was going to drop their gaze first. I was determined not to be the one to give in.

"I guess you could say that I'm this attentive with my roommates." His words were slow and methodic.

I blinked, wondering if I'd heard him right. "Excuse me?" Had he just said the word *roommate*?

He chuckled, pushed off from the wall, and made his way toward the bathroom door. Once it was open, he passed through to a door on the opposite wall. I stepped closer to see that there was a bedroom on the other side.

"I guess we're roommates now," he said.

My entire body went cold. I cleared my throat and shook my head. "There's some misunderstanding. Um…" I pushed my hands through my hair, loosening it from the bun at the nape of my neck. I hated looking disheveled, but in this moment, I didn't care. How could Maggie not tell me about this?

Sharing a bathroom was something I'd never done. And the thought of sharing it with a man who both confused and affected me was not an option.

I didn't even finish my statement. Instead, I walked straight out into the hall. Two seconds later, I was standing outside of Maggie's door, knocking.

There was some rustling, and a moment later, the door opened. Maggie was standing on the other side with her hair pulled up and a pair of red silk pajamas on. She was wearing some sort of white mask on her face, but that didn't stop her eyes from lighting up when she saw me.

"Did you get settled in?" she asked as she stepped away from the door and waved me in.

I wanted to stay in the hallway and give her a piece of my mind, but if Maggie saw that I was upset, she didn't let on. Instead, she crawled back onto her bed and proceeded to grab a chocolate from the tray next to her.

"Want one?" she asked through the chocolate in her mouth.

Knowing that it wasn't Maggie's fault and that I was really upset with Brett, I nodded and crossed the room, flopping down on the bed next to her. I ate two bonbons before I spoke.

"Why didn't you tell me that Brett and I were going to share a bathroom?"

Maggie glanced over at me, her brows furrowed. "I didn't think you'd care. You two get along well."

I pulled another bonbon from the paper but didn't eat it. Instead, I rolled it around on the palm of my hand. "Is that normal? Do all the rooms have jack and jill bathrooms?"

Maggie took a drink from the water bottle next to her. "Not really. I told you we're trying to add some rooms that can accommodate big families. You guys are staying in the first ones." She sighed as she leaned her head back. "Is it going to be a problem?"

I wanted to say yes. I wanted to demand that she put me in a different room. But I knew that she was just being nice, and I couldn't take away business from her just so that I didn't have to be this intimately connected with Brett.

Plus, this was only temporary. I was going to find my own place and a job that I loved. This was just a pit stop on the road to discovering the true Victoria.

"It's fine, I guess." I leaned back against the headboard and stared at the paused picture on the TV in front of me. I didn't recognize the characters, but from what I'd learned about Maggie, she was a Korean drama fiend.

When Maggie didn't respond right away, I glanced over to see an incredulous expression creeping across her face. It was as if she were concocting an idea in her mind that was sinister in nature. And from the looks of it, I wasn't going to like it.

"What is that look for?" I asked slowly.

She wiggled her eyebrows as she moved to sit straight up on her bed. "You like Brett." Her voice was low and breathy, but I could tell she was going to start squealing like a high school girl in a moment.

I shook my head. "No, I don't."

She didn't look convinced. Great. She was a bloodhound convinced she'd discovered a trail. "Yes, you do." She slapped her forehead with her palm. "Why didn't I see this before? You obviously like him. You get all tongue-tied when he's around." She circled her finger in the direction of my mouth.

Out of instinct, I slapped my hand over my lips and shook my head. "No, I don't," I mumbled into my palm.

She waved my comment away. "Gah, I'm really losing my touch." Then she narrowed her eyes. "Blast that Archer. He's got me distracted."

Ready to cling onto anything that wasn't my love life, I dropped my hand and plopped a melting bonbon into my mouth. "What's up with Archer?"

Maggie sighed and then glanced sideways at me. "Don't think I don't know what you're doing. Distracting me won't work. I want to talk about you and Brett."

I groaned and flopped back onto the mattress. I stared up at the ceiling. "There's not a *me and Brett*. I promise you. I see him as a blob. A non-entity." I waved my hands in and out of my vision. "I hadn't even noticed that he was a man."

Maggie's face popped into my line of sight. Her eyes were slightly narrowed. "Victoria, you can say what you want, but I don't believe you. When I think about your interactions, I can *feel* the heat." She wiggled her eyebrows. "You like him."

I groaned, covered my face with my elbow, and shook my head. "You're talking crazy," I murmured.

The feeling of the mattress shifting next to me signaled that Maggie had moved to lie down next to me. Her elbow brushed mine, but I didn't move to uncover my face.

"It's okay if you want to be in denial," she said softly.

I couldn't let what she'd said hang in the air unanswered. I dropped my arm and glanced to the side. "You're so funny," I said with a *har har* at the end.

She shrugged. "I'm pretty good at picking couples, and if I was going to bet on anyone coming together, it would be you two."

The resolution in her voice was startling. It was as if she didn't even have to think about it. It was a fact, and she was just going to sit back and wait for it to happen.

My throat tightened.

I sighed and sat up. "You're crazy." I slipped from the bed and glanced back at her.

Maggie looked so calm with her eyes closed and a soft smile on her lips. It was strange to me that she could be so calm. From what she'd told us, her life before she got to Magnolia had been a train wreck. And yet now there was no hint of her previous life. It was as if she'd found the place where she belonged.

What must that feel like?

"I'm gonna go to bed. My boss is a slave driver, and if I don't give one hundred percent, she'll have me whipped." I headed toward the door as Maggie raised her hand and made a whip cracking sound.

I laughed as I stepped out into the hallway and right into Archer. He was hunched over and holding something small and square. When he saw me, he dropped his hand to hide whatever he was looking at behind his back.

His eyes were wide when he met my gaze, and for a moment, he stood there with his lips parted and the look of death on his face. A moment later, he reached behind me to slam Maggie's door shut, then turned to stare me down.

"What did you see?"

His panic interested me, and I thought about telling him I didn't see anything, but then decided against it. He was hiding something, and I kind of wanted to know what that something was.

"I saw enough," I said as I steeled my gaze and folded my arms across my chest, accenting my words with the tapping of my fingers on my upper arm.

Archer narrowed his eyes. "You did?"

I nodded. "I did.

Silence fell around us as Archer and I participated in a good ole' fashion stare down. Just when I thought he would crack, he smiled at me. "You didn't see," he said as he pushed his hand through his floppy brown hair. "You're not a very good liar, Victoria."

I glowered at him. "I did too."

"Yeah, sure."

"I saw the ring," I said, shooting from the hip. It was the only thing that I knew came in a box that small.

Archer's expression fell as he whipped his gaze over to me. "You did see?"

Bingo. I'd guessed right.

I pinched my lips together and nodded. "You're proposing to Maggie?"

He shushed me as he pulled me into a nearby closet and shut the door. It was tight quarters, and that was only made more evident when he turned around to face me. I wanted to step back to give myself some space, but I couldn't because there was a giant mop bucket behind me.

"You've got to keep this quiet," he whispered.

I have to admit that it felt good to be privy to this information. From the complete lack of screaming coming from Clementine, I had to assume that she had no clue what Archer was going to do. That meant I was the only one on this entire island that knew what was in store for Maggie.

And for a moment, that made me feel special—even if the way I'd found out was by complete accident.

"When are you going to do it?" I asked, leaning in.

Archer studied me for a moment before he sighed. "I don't know. I'm not…" He shoved his hands into his front pockets while he shrugged. "I'm not good at this kind of stuff."

"What do you mean? You've been married. You've done it before." Just as the words left my lips, I saw Archer's face drop, and I knew that I'd made a mistake. "I'm sorry," I said, and I meant it.

Archer bounced back quickly. He shrugged and sighed. "Yeah, which is why I'm terrified to approach this subject again. What if…"

It was strange to see a man who had always been strong and aloof break down in front of me. It was a startling sight to see. Not wanting him to get too far into his head, I reached out and patted his arm.

"She loves you, Archer. She'll say yes."

Archer dropped his gaze for a moment before he nodded. "Thanks." Then he glanced back up at me. "You won't say anything, right?"

I pretended to lock my lips and throw away the key. "Mum's the word."

Archer took one last look at me before he pulled open the door. Just as he moved to step out of the closet, Archer stopped. I nearly ran into him, and it wasn't until I stepped out around him that I saw what he was looking at.

A very confused Brett was staring at the two of us.

Archer looked like he'd been caught with his hand in the cookie jar. I, on the other hand, wasn't liking the inquisitive look coming from Brett. Just as I moved to tell him off, Archer piped up.

"She saw the ring," he whispered and then hurried from the hallway, leaving me on my own to deal with the fallout.

Brett's gaze followed Archer until he disappeared. Then he turned to look at me. His eyebrows were raised, and his flirtatious smile was out—which always seemed to turn my insides into mush.

"I saw the ring," I said as if that was the answer to all of life's questions.

Brett didn't say anything. All he did was give me a "Right, sure" look and then disappear down the hallway that led to our rooms.

I let out a groan as I closed my eyes. Even though I wanted to tell Brett off, the thing running through my mind like a song on repeat was Maggie's voice telling me that I liked him.

And I was fairly certain that if I went after Brett to convince him otherwise, I would just be confirming Maggie's suspicions.

And I couldn't do that. Not right now.

And hopefully, not ever.

8

FIONA

I was on edge Sunday and Monday. After Shari gave me her brother-in-law's information, I left him a voice message asking him to call me back. I knew it was unrealistic to think that he would call me right away Monday morning, but when noon rolled around, and he still hadn't called, I was a mess.

Every sound my phone made caused me to jump. Whether it was a text or an email notification, I found myself running to find out what it was.

So when my phone rang at twelve thirty, I was exhausted. Not even looking, I brought my phone to my cheek. I had ten minutes left of my break before I had to go back out and serve coffee once more.

"Hello?" I asked.

"Hello? Fiona?"

I sat up straight in my chair. "Yes, this is Fiona."

The man cleared his throat. "Great. This is Austin. Shari asked me to give you a call, and I got your voicemail. Sorry it's taken me a while to get back with you, but I've been swamped here."

I shook my head. I had no right to complain. He was going to give me free legal advice. I shouldn't have been so impatient.

"Oh, no. That's okay. I didn't expect you to call me back this soon."

He chuckled. "That's good, then. So, what can I do for you?"

I sucked in my breath and then told him my situation. He marked every few sentences of mine with a "mm-hmm" or an "I understand." By the time I was done, he was so quiet that I feared I'd lost connection.

"Well, Fiona, I would say if you don't have money for a lawyer and you think that Dave will be amenable, I would suggest you start with just talking to him. It's better for Blake and better for you emotionally if you can come to an agreement on your own. After that, things get touchy. Feelings can get hurt, and I've seen relationships get ruined."

My heart began to hammer in my chest. That was not what I wanted for me or for Blake—but mostly Blake. He deserved so much better.

"Do you think that is something you can do?" he asked.

I chewed on my bottom lip as I attempted to calm the butterflies that had taken flight in my stomach. "I think I can do that. After all, we didn't really part on bad terms, just a *'see ya later'* kind of thing."

Austin clicked his tongue. "That's good to know. If it doesn't work, reach out to me again, and I can lay out the next steps." The sound of a phone ringing in the background had him speaking again. "That's a phone call I've been waiting on. I've got to go."

"Okay."

"Call me if you need any more help," he said before the phone went quiet.

I sat there for a moment with my phone pressed to my ear. My body felt numb as the silence of the room engulfed me. I didn't want to contact Dave, but I also knew that it needed to happen if I was going to be able to help Mom. She needed every dollar she could get, and since she was paying for me and Blake, I needed to contribute what I could.

"Who was that?"

Mom's voice startled me. I swung my feet off the desk in front of me and hurried to stand. She had her arms folded and an eyebrow raised. She looked inquisitive, not mad. So my worry that she had heard too much was lessened.

"Just a solicitor," I said as I slipped my phone into the back pocket of my jeans.

Mom didn't look convinced, but she didn't let it linger for long. Instead, she nodded and motioned toward the dining room. "Ready to get back? I need a break. My feet are killing me."

I nodded and gathered up my garbage. Then I paused in the doorway as I watched Mom collapse on the chair I'd just vacated. When she leaned forward and rested her head on her outstretched arm, guilt washed over me.

I could tell that she was tired, and I knew I was the cause of it. Seeing her exhausted just solidified inside of me the need to do all I could to get Dave helping out with Blake. I needed to find another job, so I could take care of my son and my mom.

After Mom's break, she came into the shop to tell me that she wasn't feeling well. She asked if I could handle things on my own. Not wanting to disappoint her, I said I could cover things. Blake was doing well in the corner of the shop, and it was a Monday, so it was quiet.

Mom nodded slowly and said to come wake her in an hour. I ushered her upstairs and then plopped down next to Blake with a coloring book and some markers.

We spent the next half an hour coloring and listening to baby songs. There was the occasional Magnolia resident who popped in for a coffee. They were polite, talking to Blake as he grunted and kept his focus on his show.

By four, Mom still hadn't come down, and I didn't have the heart to go wake her up. Blake was happily munching on some fries from the burgers that I'd had delivered when the door opened, and Shari came walking in. Bella and Tag were following behind her, dragging their feet as she pulled them inside.

"I don't want to, Mom," Tag whined.

Shari gave out an exasperated sigh, but when she saw me, she broke out into a smile. "Oh, good, you're here."

I nodded as I moved to stand. Once I was behind the counter, Shari ordered her kids to sit by Blake—who was suddenly very interested in the big kids that had surrounded him—and leaned over the counter.

"Austin said you called him," she said, her voice low.

I was busy getting her change for the three smoothies and two cookies she'd ordered. I nodded as I handed the money over to her. "Yeah, we just got off the phone."

Shari immediately dumped her change into the tip jar as she moved with me over to the blenders. "What did he say?"

I glanced over my shoulder as I pulled out the frozen fruit. "Did he not tell you?"

Shari shook her head. "No. He was tight as a drum." She shrugged. "I guess that means he's a good lawyer or something."

I chuckled. "I guess being tight-lipped is kind of a professional hazard."

Shari puffed up her cheeks before she blew out her breath. "Yeah. So…" She circled her hand in front of her as if to tell me to spill it.

I shrugged, ran the blender for a moment, and then turned to face her as I poured the banana and strawberry smoothie into a cup. "He said I should talk to Dave. That if we have a good relationship, then we should try to make the arrangements ourselves." I set the empty blender into the sink and then retrieved a lid from the stack and popped it onto the cup.

"So, did you?"

I paused. The chill of the frozen mixed berries startled me. "Not yet," I finally said as I dumped the fruit into another blender.

"Why not?"

I ran the blender and then filled another glass. "I don't know. I haven't talked to him in about a year. I'm not even sure if I have his number anymore." I popped the lid on and stuck a straw into it. "I was going to do some digging tonight once Blake is in bed."

Shari shook her head. Her quick dismissal of my plan confused me.

"What?" I asked.

She leaned forward on her elbows, wagging her finger in front of me. "You're not going to do it if you tackle it like that. Trust me, I know what avoidance looks like, and this is avoidance." She pushed off the counter and glanced around the room. "Where's your phone?"

I swallowed. I'd grown to see Shari as a friend, but I didn't like what she was doing. I was determined to make this work, but I wanted to do it on my terms. Even if she felt like I was moving at glacier speed.

"Blake has it." I nodded toward the table where Blake was holding my phone in the air as if it were his prized possession.

Shari clicked her tongue and then, a moment later, crossed the room and asked Blake for the phone. I half expected him to clutch it to his chest and reject her, but to my dismay, he didn't. Instead, he happily handed it over to her and then settled down next to Tag, who was pulling up something on his phone.

I watched in amazement as Shari walked back over to me with the phone extended in front of her. "There," she said as she set it down in front of me. "Easy peasy."

"What sort of dark magic do you hold?" I asked as I gave her a look before picking up my phone.

Shari shrugged. "I have an aura about me. I work with kids all day, and even though I don't have my own figured out, I'd say I'm pretty good at my job."

I raised my finger. "I'm putting you on retainer. Whenever I need help defusing a Blake situation, I'm calling you."

Shari looked over her shoulder at my son. "What are you talking about? He's adorable."

I scoffed as I swiped my phone on. "He's cute now, but come bath time, dinner time, nap time, or bedtime…" I raised my eyebrows, and Shari laughed.

"I get it. Mom here, too." Then she wrinkled her nose. "Except when they are preteens. They get less difficult about bath or dinner time, but I think bedtime will be a struggle."

I laughed and nodded. "Yeah. I'm excited for him to get older, but at the same time, I'm not."

Our laughter drifted off to silence, and I noticed Shari was staring at me. She dropped her gaze to my phone and then back up to me. I could feel her expectation.

She wanted me to find out about Dave. And no matter what excuse I tried to come up with, nothing was going to sound good. Everything would ring hollow in the air.

I was going to track down my ex whether I wanted to or not.

I located the last phone number I had for him and pressed talk. Then I waited for the ringtone to come through.

Nothing.

Suddenly, an error message blared into my ear and a robotic woman told me that the number I was trying to reach had been disconnected. My stomach fell as I dropped my hand to the counter. Then I shrugged at Shari—she had the same defeated look as I did.

"I guess he changed his number," I said. It hurt, the idea that Dave had moved on without me. I was his ex after all. We had a son together. He could have let me know if he was moving. He should have let me know.

Here I was thinking we had a relationship when, in fact, we didn't. I was probably reading too much into this, but how else was I supposed to look at it? He'd severed the only line of communication I had with him.

It made our separation that much more poignant.

"Is there anyone you can call or text?"

I swallowed against the lump in my throat and shrugged. "Maybe? I had his sister's number once." I scrolled through my contacts and landed on Kimberly's name. "I could text her."

Shari nodded. "Do it."

I glanced up at her and sighed. Shari was going to push me out of my comfort zone whether I wanted her to or not.

Great.

Me: Hey, Kim, it's Fiona. I need to get ahold of Dave. It's about Blake. Do you have his number?

I sent off the text. Feeling antsy, I finished blending up the last smoothie and then handed the tray filled with the treats and smoothies to Shari. It wasn't until she left to bring the food to the table that my phone chimed.

My stomach lurched as I flipped my phone over to stare at the screen.

Kim had texted me back.

Kim: I don't. He cut me off a while ago. We had a fight—long story. I do know that he's still in Nashville if that helps.

A defeated feeling filled my body. This was going to be harder than I'd thought. Maybe this was foolish. Maybe I should just give up and find another job. I'm sure there was *something* I could do that didn't require bringing Dave back into my life.

"Any response?" Shari asked as she stepped up to the counter. She was holding her smoothie and taking the occasional sip.

I slid my phone across the countertop, and she caught it. After a quick read, she glanced up at me.

"Well, that stinks," she said as she pushed it back. "And there's no one else?"

I shrugged. "If he's cut his sister out of his life, I'm guessing he's ditched all of our old friends."

"Do you know where he would be in Nashville?"

I leaned my hip against the counter and folded my arms. I had a sinking suspicion as to where Shari was going with this, but I wasn't sure I wanted to play this game. "Maybe? I mean, I know our old apartment and the bars he'd play. That's assuming he hasn't moved on."

"Is he good enough to play at different bars?"

I honestly had no idea. When I was with Dave, I'd been obsessed with him. Anything he created sounded amazing. I hadn't stuck around long enough to know if his music was still great once I no longer cared about him. I split the first chance I got.

"What do you want to do?" Shari asked. I could tell by the slow way she spoke she was gauging my reaction.

I studied her. "I don't know. Part of me wants to head down there to find him. The other part wants to just give up. I mean, I've gotten this far without him. Do I really need him?"

Shari studied me for a moment before she glanced behind her at the kids. Then she sighed and turned to face me. "I know what you are going through, Fiona. I went through the same thing. We are more similar than you think." She smiled softly. "Men have hurt our families. And it sucks that we still have to be the adults in the situation."

Tears brimmed my eyes. No one had spoken to me like this before. Everyone just assumed since I was young and stupid and had *made* the choice to go with him, that I should just buck up and deal with the hand I was dealt. It was strange to have someone take my side for a change.

Strange and startling.

Shari popped into my gaze. Her eyebrows were furrowed as she studied me. "You okay, Fiona?"

I blinked a few times before I nodded. "Yeah. I am." I

wiped my cheeks just to make sure that I hadn't been crying and then shifted my focus to what she had said. "So what do you think I should do?"

Shari tapped her chin. Then she glanced around before she leaned in. "I think it's time for a road trip."

VICTORIA

Brett was unusually chipper when I walked into the kitchen on Tuesday morning. As soon as our gazes met, he smiled at me. Not in a friendly kind of way, but in a mysterious I-just-might-murder-you kind of way. I paused in the doorway and eyed him.

"You look happy today," I said as I slipped my purse off my shoulder and hung it on the hook next to the door. Then I pulled out the apron that Brett had given me and slipped it over my head.

Thankfully, yesterday was full of checkouts and cleaning rooms. Maggie told me that was normal for a Monday. So I didn't spend any time in the kitchen with Brett. Besides passing in the halls, we really hadn't seen each other since Saturday night. I hadn't been here on Sunday because I'd needed to start packing my room for the move.

Even sharing a bathroom with Brett proved to be less of

a problem than I'd anticipated. He kept to himself, and honestly neither of us spent that much time in the bathroom, which meant we rarely saw each other.

I felt a tad ridiculous that I'd freaked out the way I did. It wasn't a good color on me, and it gave Maggie the license to give me goofy smiles every time Brett and I were in the same room, but that was about it. I just smiled back at her. After all, I knew a secret about her that she didn't know. And even though I'd promised Archer complete silence on the subject, it didn't change the fact that I knew Maggie's life was going to change very soon.

With that little hiccup out of the way, I was gaining confidence that moving into the inn for the short term was a positive thing for me. Plus, it made Mom and Dad more confused since I hadn't been there to fight with them. I was loving the independence. This is what my life should have been like from the beginning.

Adults were meant to leave the house of their parents.

Brett chuckled as he grabbed a freshly fried doughnut and handed it to me. Without thinking, I grabbed it as it dropped into my hand. The warm sugar glaze slipped between my fingers, and suddenly my stomach was growling. I bit into the warm doughnut and let out a sigh.

"I'm going to have to buy a whole new wardrobe," I said as I licked the icing from my fingers. With Brett cooking every meal, I was fairly certain my waistline was going to steadily expand.

Brett chuckled. "I think that might be a good thing."

I eyed him. What did that mean? I glanced down at my white button-down shirt that was tucked into my navy-blue dress slacks. "What's wrong with what I'm wearing?"

Brett dumped the mixing bowl he'd just emptied into the warm, sudsy sink and then glanced over his shoulder at me. He took his time as he swept his gaze over me. He started at my feet and then made his way all the way up to my hair. Feeling nervous, I moved to tuck my hair behind my ear only to realize that I still had glaze on my fingers, and it was now stuck to the strands of my hair.

Brett must have realized my mistake because, a moment later, he stepped up to me with a dishcloth in hand. He didn't hesitate as me moved close to me, gently taking my hair into his hand. He smelled like sugar and summer rain. It was a confusing combination, but it made me want to take a deep breath. It made me want to breathe him in.

I blinked, trying to remove that desire from my mind as I watched him gently blot my hair. His gaze remained focused on what he was doing even though I was fairly certain I was staring at him.

"It's not that what you wear is bad," he finally said. He paused before he glanced over at me. It wasn't until he was studying me that I realized just how close our bodies were. All I needed to do was lean in and our lips would touch.

That thought caused an ache to rise up inside of me. I wanted to be touched. It had been too long since a man had wrapped me in his arms.

"It's not?" I whispered. I couldn't control my racing

heart, so I shouldn't have been surprised that my tone of voice followed suit.

He shook his head. "I just don't think that it's you."

His words confused me. I furrowed my brow as I stared at him. He thought that dress slacks and pressed blouses weren't me? They were definitely me. His claim reminded me that we'd just met. Whomever he thought Victoria was, she wasn't the real me.

And that thought worried me.

He raised his hand and took a step back. Instantly, I felt cold in his absence. I wanted to follow him. Being this close to a man opened a desire inside of myself that I thought had died, but I also didn't want to be weak.

If I allowed myself to fall for him, how long would that last? It was only a matter of time before he discovered the real Victoria, and he would want to leave. Just like everyone else.

"Why don't you think my clothes are me?" Even though I knew I should walk away, there was something holding me to this spot. Perhaps I was just too stubborn to have someone in this town thinking they knew more about me than I did. Or maybe I was intrigued by what he saw in me.

How it could be completely different from what I saw in myself?

Brett glanced down at his clasped hands. He'd deposited the washcloth into the sink and was now fiddling with his fingers. I couldn't tell if he was weighing his words or if he was teasing me.

Regardless, his coyness was driving me crazy.

"I don't think you know who Victoria is." He glanced up. His gaze was warm and inviting even if it felt as if his words were attacking me.

"You think I don't know who Victoria is?" I repeated, just to make sure I'd heard him right.

He raised his hands. "It's not that I think I know you better. It's just that when I saw you at the inauguration, and even when Maggie dragged you in here, you didn't look like you knew what you wanted." He shrugged. "I know the feeling."

Even though I wanted to fight him, to tell him that he was wrong, I couldn't. There was a truth to his words, and even though they hurt me, I couldn't ignore them. His words broke down the wall that I had built up inside of me. The one that I'd used to protect me from everyone else.

Perhaps it was his honesty. Or maybe it was the vulnerability in the way he stared at me and in the words he used that made me want to let him in ever so slightly.

"So how did you figure out what you wanted?" My words were raspy, and I could hear the emotion in my voice.

Brett's expression relaxed as his half smile returned. It was faint, but I could see the corner of his lips tip up. It sent a wave of pleasure through my body. The fact that I could get him to smile affected me in a way that I hadn't expected.

"Do you really want to know?"

I nodded.

He paused before he clicked his tongue and pointed his forefinger at me. "I'm not going to tell you."

Like touching a needle to a blown-up balloon, the anticipation inside of me fizzled. I glared at him and was hot on his heels as he made his way into the side pantry. "You're not going to tell me?" Why did my temperature feel so elevated right now? I was used to men playing with my emotions. I was used to having people lead me on only to drop me.

Why was I so bothered that Brett would do the same?

Brett reached to the top shelf and removed a clean platter. Then he turned, stopping right before he ran into me. His mischievous smile was back as he sidestepped me. I hurried after him as he walked over to the fryer and began stacking warm doughnuts on the platter.

"Well?"

He glanced back over at me. "I'll tell you while we work."

I glared at him, but when I realized that he wasn't looking, I sighed and made my way over to the sink. After my hands were cleaned, I began helping him with the few remaining doughnuts.

"Well?" I asked again, glancing up to see his lips twitching.

How he could be so aggravating and yet so attractive was a mystery to me.

"I'm not going to tell you because I think you'll understand better if I show you." He wiped his hands on his apron and moved to pick up the full platter.

I grabbed a nearby dish towel and removed the sticky sugar from my fingers. "Show me? Show me what?"

Carrying the platter with both hands, Brett moved toward the swinging door that separated the kitchen from the dining room.

"I guess you'll just have to meet me in the bathroom tonight."

Before I could respond, Brett was gone. The door swung back and forth a few times after his departure. I glared at the door, imagining where Brett was on the other side before I sighed, scrubbed my face with my hands, and took in a deep breath.

"Wow. The tension in here is intense."

I turned to see Maggie step out of the office in the far corner of the kitchen with a giant grin on her face. I glared at her, but she just brushed it off.

"There is no tension," I lied. It was getting pathetic, in fact. She was able to pick up on it from the other room. I was headed for some serious trouble.

Maggie snorted. "Oh, okay, I'm just taking crazy pills."

I clicked my tongue as I shot a finger pistol in her direction. "Yep, that was what I was going to say."

Maggie chuckled as she moved to grab a water bottle from the fridge. "I don't know why you are fighting it. After all, he likes you. A lot."

My cheeks warmed. My throat felt as if it were closing. And for a moment I wondered if I were having an allergic reaction to the doughnut he'd fed me. But that feeling dissipated, and I was left with the realization that her words gave me hope. That they stirred a feeling inside of me that I wasn't sure I liked.

"You think so?" I mumbled. I couldn't help myself. I wanted to hear it from someone else. Sure, I'd picked up on his sexy smiles and flirtatious comments, but that didn't mean they were real or that I was interpreting them right.

Maggie nodded. "Oh, yeah. Brett is interested. With all the women I've seen show up here, I've never seen him react the way he does to you."

I blinked. "Women?"

Maggie nodded before her expression morphed into humiliation. She slammed her hand over her lips and shook her head. "I'm sorry. I didn't mean it like that. Brett doesn't have a lot of women come here." She sighed and shrugged. "I guess they just follow him. Most are from the club across the bridge."

Great. Now I was contending with twenty-year-olds. This day was just getting crappier and crappier.

"Good to know," I said as I turned to head over to the sink where Brett had discarded the dishes that needed to be washed. I flipped the faucet on and let it run into the sudsy water.

"Victoria, I don't think he's a womanizer." Maggie was right behind me. She rested her hand on my shoulder, but I shrugged it off.

"I know that." I scoffed. I didn't picture him as that kind of guy. But that didn't mean that I was the woman for him. After all, why would he pick a high-strung, incredibly tense type A personality when he could have a fawn-all-over-you woman?

I was a lot of work. And the girls you find at clubs? Well, they weren't exactly the make-you-work-for-it kind of women. No man in his right mind would stick around for a woman who was work.

This was a fact. One that had been made clear one too many times in my dating history.

"Just forget what I said, okay? And go back to being happy."

I could hear the desperation in Maggie's voice. She was genuinely worried that she'd ruined something for me. I didn't like that she felt that way. Not when I knew it wouldn't have been long before I ruined things myself. Her panic made me feel like a terrible person.

"I'm happy," I said as I forced a smile and turned to face her. She studied me, and I could tell that she didn't believe me, but after a few moments, she nodded.

"I just don't want to ruin this for you. I'm excited, and sometimes I stick my foot in my mouth."

I swirled the dishrag around in the bubbles. My mind was too distracted to do the dishes. "You can't ruin anything when there's nothing to ruin."

"Mags?"

Archer's voice drew our attention over to the back door. He was standing there looking more panicked than normal. I wondered if this was the moment he was going to propose, but from his dirty hands and sweaty brow, I hoped that wasn't the case.

"Coming," Maggie sang out before she turned to face me. "Don't let what I said change your feelings for Brett. You deserve to be happy."

I nodded and then tipped my head in Archer's direction. "You should go."

She gave me one last worried look before she nodded and left me alone with the pile of dishes. I focused my attention on washing the batter from the utensils, allowing myself to get lost in the feeling of accomplishment that came from completing simple tasks.

I took in a deep breath and let it out slowly just as Brett's face popped up next to me. He was grinning once more as he leaned into my line of sight and wiggled my eyebrows.

"I've never seen someone stare so longingly at a sink full of dishes before," he said as he moved to lean one arm on the countertop next to me.

I finished wiping the mixer blade before I rinsed it and stuck it in the drying rack next to me. There was so much that I wanted to say to him, but I wasn't sure how. I feared that anything that escaped from my lips would sound like flirting, and that was the last thing I wanted to do.

I needed to keep my distance from him, and allowing myself to slip into these little tiffs with him was not the way to do that.

"I'm just making sure I do a good job." I shook off the excess water from the pot I'd just washed and placed it upside down on the drying board, so the water could drip off. I gave Brett a wide grin as I moved on.

He just kept smiling at me as I worked. Not sure what to do, I decided that staying focused on my job was best. Until, that is, it became apparent that he had no intention of leaving my side.

I turned to face him. "Everything okay?"

He grabbed an apple from the bowl next to him and bit into it. Then he nodded as he chewed thoughtfully. "I'm just excited for tonight. Be prepared to let your hair down."

Fear crept up inside of me as he gave me a wink and turned away. He hummed as he walked over to the cupboard of recipes books and grabbed one out. He plopped down at the small table in the corner and began thumbing through it.

I swallowed as I turned my attention back to the dishes. He was excited, and it made me nervous. I wasn't sure I was going to like what he was going to make me do. He seemed confident that he knew me, and he was going to bring out a side of me that I hadn't allowed to exist.

But that wasn't what scared me the most. What scared me above all was that, at the end of this, I was going to like the woman I became when I was with him more than I liked the woman I was now.

And that was a lot of eggs to put into one basket.

What if he discovered he really wasn't interested in the Victoria Holt he was convinced I was hiding?

What if he decided to leave and I was left alone?

How would I move on from that?

I shook my head as I popped a few bubbles in the water. I wouldn't. There wasn't any moving on from that.

I would break. More than I already was. And at that point I was fairly certain there would be no putting me back together again.

I wasn't sure if I was willing to take that risk.

There was too much at stake.

10

VICTORIA

I don't know why I was nervous. I felt stupid, standing in my room, debating if I should tell Brett that I was sick or if I should just ghost him all together. My stomach was in knots, and I was fairly certain that I just might puke up the sausage gravy and biscuits he'd made for dinner.

If that happened, I'd have all the proof I needed to get out of whatever Brett had planned for tonight.

Just as I was about to crawl out of my clothes and into my pajamas, there was a knock on my door. I started at it, wondering if I wished hard enough, could I make it Maggie standing on the other side?

I winced as the person knocked again. From the strong cadence, I knew that it wasn't Maggie. It was Brett, and he wasn't going away. So I sighed, fluffed my hair, and crossed the room.

I opened the door mid knock, and he stood there with

his eyebrows raised, studying me. I had hoped that he would be dressed in a way that clued me in on what we were doing, but I had no such luck. He had on a flannel shirt with jeans and boots. His normal daily attire. Well, at least we weren't headed to some fancy restaurant. I could cross that off the list in my head.

"We're still on?" I asked as I opened my door wider.

Brett's smile didn't falter as he walked into my room. I hadn't invited him in, and yet he strode in like he owned the place. "Come with me," he said as he opened my door to our bathroom and crossed over to his side.

It felt strange, seeing how close we were to each other. The only thing separating us was a six-inch wall. It was nerve-racking, and I couldn't help it when my mind wandered to what that meant for us.

I shook my head. Nothing. It meant nothing. Because there was no us. I was the ridiculous idiot who seemed to think that there might be something going on between us when I knew very well there wasn't.

I was making things up in my mind that were going to lead to my demise.

"What's in there?" I asked as I lingered in my doorway. I hadn't crossed the threshold that led to his room. It was small, but I had to hold onto the last bit of control that I felt I had.

Brett popped into view with a mysterious smile on his lips. I was beginning to realize that every time that smile appeared, I was in trouble.

"Come in here and you'll find out," he said. There was a

hint to his tone that caused my heart rate to pick up. My stomach lightened as I focused my vision into his room as if it held the answers to my questions. Brett shook his head. "You need to learn to live a little."

I glared back at him. I knew what he said was true, but I wasn't quite ready to take that leap. I took a breath and marched over to his bedroom. When I got inside, I glanced around. It was larger than mine. A queen-size bed sat along one side of the wall. It was decorated in soft yellows and tans just like mine.

It didn't look like the manly room I'd expected. Instead, it looked undisturbed. As if this wasn't the place he was meant to settle down in—just like me.

"Like what you see?" Brett asked. He'd moved over to the bed and was leaning against one of the posts.

Not wanting him to ask me any further questions, I shrugged as I reached out and ran my fingers against the smooth wood of his dresser. "It's nice. Not what I expected from you. But this is Maggie's inn. I'm not sure why I thought it would be different."

"You've been picturing my room?"

My entire body heated from his question. I glanced behind me as I cursed the fact that my cheeks were on fire. I swallowed and offered a meager, "No."

Brett just chuckled and shrugged. "I wouldn't blame you. Most women do."

His last words lingered in the air. I blinked a few times, wondering how I was supposed to respond to that. My conversation with Maggie rose in my mind, and suddenly I felt very vulnerable.

I was allowing myself to like a man who spent most of his time at work around drunk women. I needed to remember that. Brett may be good at flirting, but was he good at relationships? My gut told me no. And even though my gut had made some questionable decisions in the past, I was willing to trust it this time.

"Did I say something wrong?"

Brett pulled me from my thoughts. I turned to see that he had moved to grab a pile of clothes. Not wanting him to be privy to my thoughts, I shrugged and shook my head. "Nope. What are those for?"

His smile widened. "These are for you. You need to wear them for what we are going to do."

I eyed the clothes. From what I could tell, it was a flannel shirt and a pair of jeans—just like his. "Why?" I asked, drawing out the word.

"You'll just have to trust me."

Ooo, that word. Trust. Thing was, I didn't trust people. Everyone I knew always seemed to want to stab me in the back. And a sexy, mysterious man that I couldn't read? He was the most dangerous of all.

"I don't know…"

He stepped forward as he focused his gaze on me. His presence sent a wave of warmth over my body. "I promise you'll enjoy yourself."

There was something about the way he was staring at me, daring me to trust him, that caused the wall I had built up inside of me to crumble. The will to keep him at a distance was failing, and suddenly all I wanted to do was throw on these ridiculous clothes and ride off with him on his white steed.

"Okay," I whispered. That seemed to be what he needed to hear. He dropped the clothes into my outstretched hands and then waved toward our bathroom.

I walked into it and shut the door. After a few seconds of regret, I pushed my fear aside and slipped into what he'd picked out for me. After tying the bottom of the shirt in a knot in front of me, I glanced in the mirror. The girl that was staring back at me looked different. It wasn't the same put together Victoria that I was used to.

She looked comfortable. Relaxed. It was strange that a flannel shirt and a pair of loose-fitting pants could make me feel this way. The worry that I didn't look sexy passed through my head, but then I pushed it out. After all, I wasn't here to woo Brett. I was here because he asked me to come, and I figured he wouldn't leave me alone if I didn't.

It was really self-preservation that had me here.

I opened the bathroom door and headed back into Brett's room. He was busy on his phone, so he didn't see me right away. But as soon as he raised his gaze, my entire body flushed. There was a look in his eyes. I couldn't pinpoint what it was, but I swear I saw desire.

My heart began to race as I lifted my arms and turned. I needed to break his stare by any means possible. "They're big, but I'm wearing them," I said as I hiked up the loose pants.

Brett slipped his phone into his pocket and stood. "They look great."

I shrugged as I folded the top band of the pants down. That helped tighten the jeans on my hips. "So where are we going? A farm?"

He moved to grab his wallet and keys from the dresser next to me. Just as he did, I caught a whiff of his cologne. There was something calming and familiar about it. I needed to find out what it was, so I could go out and buy a bottle. Then I wouldn't be trying to sniff him. Instead, I could enjoy it in the privacy of my own home.

Thankfully, he didn't seem to notice me leaning in. He pulled back and gave me a big smile. "Where we're going is for me to know and for you to find out."

Fifteen minutes into our drive, I still had no idea where we were going. The sun was officially tucked behind the horizon, and the only thing I could see was a faint glow from where it had been. I glanced out the rolled down window. The smell of the salt that filled the air had me relaxing in my seat.

I was home. This was home. All the stress of the week melted away, and I was left with a sense of being that I'd never felt before. It was strange, but in this moment, I welcomed it.

Brett was humming along with the soft ballad playing on the radio, and for a moment, I glanced over at him. He looked so peaceful, driving down the road, the wind from the open windows ruffling his hair.

What was he thinking about? Was it me? Was he happy

to be this close to me? I wanted him to be. I wanted this moment to mean something to him.

Because he was slowly beginning to mean something to me.

"I'm going to melt under your stare," he said as he reached forward and flicked off the music. He took a moment to glance in my direction before he turned his attention back to the road. Then he reached forward into his cup holder, and suddenly, a penny landed in my lap. "A penny for your thoughts?"

I picked up the coin and turned it around in my fingers. I rubbed the smooth metal as I contemplated what I wanted to say. How honest I wanted to be.

"Why are you doing this?" finally tumbled from my lips. I pinched them together, hoping I hadn't offended him. But I truly wanted to know what his angle was. It couldn't be that he wanted to spend time with me. There had to be an ulterior motive.

Brett squeezed the steering wheel and relaxed his grip a few times. Then he shrugged. "I know what you're going through. I've been there myself."

I did not expect that answer. "What do you mean?"

He shrugged. "Harvard Law School. Class of '05."

My shock was growing stronger. "You're a lawyer?"

He nodded. "And my dad. And his dad. And his dad." He glanced over at me. "It's kind of a family tradition."

I mouthed the word *wow*.

"Shocking. I know. Most women can't believe that a guy as handsome as me wasn't a model in another life."

I scoffed. "It's not that."

"Oh, so you don't think I'm handsome?"

I blinked. "What? No."

"So you think I'm handsome."

I was thoroughly confused. How had we gotten here? "Um, yes?"

He glanced over at me again. "Was that a question?"

"Yes?" Then I shook my head. "No?" Why was my brain short-circuiting right now? How had I forgotten how to formulate words?

"Harvard," I finally managed out.

He chuckled. "Sorry. Had to take a moment to tease you before we get into the thick of my past." He sighed. "Yes, Harvard."

"How does a lawyer go from one of the most prestigious law schools in the country to working as a bartender and a chef at a local inn?"

Suddenly, he flipped on his blinker and pulled into a small parking lot that lined the beach. I glanced out the window at our surroundings.

He turned off the engine and killed the headlights. Then he leaned forward with his lips tipped up. "We're here," he said. I wasn't sure if he was trying to be sinister, but that's how it came out.

"Is this where you're going to kill me?" I asked—only half joking.

He shrugged. "I guess you'll have to follow me to find out." He unbuckled his seatbelt, pulled the keys from the ignition, and climbed out. Then he dipped back down so he could see me. "I'll answer more questions if you follow me." He marked the end of his sentence with the slam of his door.

I watched him move to the back of the car and pull open the trunk. A moment later, he emerged with two coolers stacked on top of each other. He then made his way to the sand, climbing over a dune and disappearing down the other side.

My desire to stay here and not do whatever crazy thing he had planned soon gave out. I growled as I pulled open the door and followed. After a few seconds of sand spilling into my shoes, I kicked them off and tucked them under my arm as I ran after him.

By the time I caught up to him, he'd spread out a blanket on the sand. The sound of the waves crashing into the shore filled my ears. The salty wind whipped around me, making me feel both warm and cold at the same time. It was a strange sensation.

"Oh, good. You're here."

I shrugged as I shoved my hands into my pockets. "You told me to follow you."

He glanced up before he started sifting around in one of the coolers. "You're brave."

"I have questions."

He chuckled as he started piecing together a fishing pole. "Well, you came to the right place."

I eyed the pole. "We're fishing?"

He nodded. "And cooking our food here." He nodded toward the small stack of wood next to the blanket.

"I stink at fishing, just to warn you."

He finished threading a hook on the line and then added what looked like chopped up fish. "Well, it's a good thing I'm here." He flexed his muscles. "I was named champion fisher during my eighth-grade summer camping trip."

I raised my eyebrows. "So my dinner plans hinge on your success from years ago?"

He laughed, the wind picking up the sound and surrounding me with it. Even though I hated the look and smell of raw fish, his laughter made me smile. Everything about Brett made me smile. I liked spending time with him, and I liked that he seemed to enjoy spending time with me.

We attempted to fish for the next hour. By the time I collapsed on the blanket, I was tired and hungry. Brett was determined to catch something even though his pants were drenched from getting too close to the ocean and a wave overtaking him. I sighed as I watched him reel in the line only to discover that he'd caught seaweed…again.

"Give it up," I called out to him. I stretched out my back before I reached forward and fisted some of the sand in my hand. I had to admit I liked that Brett was determined. He was focused—like me—and that made me respect him all the more.

Plus, it helped me relate to him on a level that I hadn't thought possible for me. Most men were intimidated by my success. If they weren't attempting to push me down, they were making me feel guilty for working hard.

But Brett seemed perfectly fine with letting me be me. And it was as refreshing as it was terrifying. I didn't know how to handle it, and I could feel my walls fortifying around my heart. If I let him in, I wasn't sure what he was going to do. Not knowing was terrifying, to say the least.

Ten minutes later, Brett gave up. He turned and shrugged as he secured the hook to the pole and walked through the sand over to where I sat. I raised my eyebrows as he shoved the pole down into the sand and then collapsed next to me.

"No fish?" I asked as I brushed my hands against each other, allowing the bits of sand to fall around me.

He shook his head. "That's okay though. I've got some snacks here."

I dropped my jaw. "You've held out on me all this time?"

I reached out to swat his arm. Just as I neared his shoulder, Brett reached out and grabbed my hand. His grip was firm and warm, and his gaze was downturned to study our hands.

He held my fingers in his for a moment before he relaxed his grip and allowed my fingers to linger against his palm. "You have feminine hands," he whispered.

I wasn't sure why the tone of his voice had changed, but I could hear the noticeable shift. It was as if touching me caused a reaction in him. I wanted to believe that, but I wasn't sure what would happen if I embraced it fully.

Needing to take a moment to gather my thoughts, I pulled my hand back and tucked it under my knees. Then I shrugged. "Thanks, I guess," I said softly.

Brett paused, and I feared that I'd said something wrong.

But then he clapped his hands and rose up onto his knees, pulling the nearest cooler closer to him.

"I'm starving," he said as he started pulling crackers and containers of fruit from inside.

It didn't take long before we were munching on the food while a fire crackled next to us. The warmth it gave off was nice, but I found myself leaning closer and closer to another heat source—Brett.

The feeling of his hand on mine and the heat I felt when he was near made me wonder what it might feel like to be wrapped up in his arms.

And the more time I spent with him, the stronger that desire was.

I feared that if I didn't start backing away now, I was only going to fall deeper down the rabbit hole that was Brett.

It might have sounded exciting, but things had a way of turning on me.

He was nice now, but eventually, he'd run. And once he did, I'd be left like I always was.

Alone and forgotten.

FIONA

I stood next to my beat-up Volkswagen Bug, watching the numbers on the gas pump increase. My stomach was still in knots even though it had been over ten hours since Shari and I had left Magnolia. The last day had been a whirlwind. After Shari decided that we needed to head to Tennessee to track down Dave, she took the reins of this operation.

Child care was arranged for Blake. Shari requested time off of work. And suddenly, my bags were packed, I kissed Blake goodbye, and we were on our way. Now I was standing next to my car watching the numbers tick up and wondering if I had done the right thing.

Was any of this the right thing?

What if Dave didn't want to be tracked down? What if when I walked up to him, he had his life together, had a girlfriend, and I was the only one who was drowning?

I couldn't see my ex like this. Not with my life hanging

on by a thread and with nowhere to turn but to the one man who broke my heart.

When had my life become so pathetic?

"You okay?" Shari asked.

I turned to see her walking over with two hot dogs and two sodas in hand. She waited for a white van to drive by before she hurried over to me. I took one soda and one hot dog from her as she turned to lean against the driver's door.

I sighed and nodded. "I'm just worried."

Shari was mid bite on her hot dog, but her eyes never left my face. After she finished chewing, she licked her lips. "Danny will do great with Blake. He loves kids."

I shook my head. Even though I was skeptical about Danny Holt watching my only son, that wasn't what had my stomach aching and the little voice inside of my head telling me that I was making a huge mistake. "Not about that."

Shari took another bite and chewed thoughtfully. "Dave? You're worried about him?"

I picked at the bun of my hot dog just as the gas pump clicked off. I set the food onto the roof of my car and moved to take care of the pump. Once the gas cap was on and the door closed, I retrieved my food from the roof and hurried over to the passenger door.

Thankfully, Shari insisted on driving. I wondered if she was worried that I might lose my nerve and flip a U-turn back to Magnolia. She wouldn't be wrong if she thought that. After all, that idea was playing in my mind like a skipping cd.

After the engine was started and we were back on the

freeway, I sighed and forced myself to take a bite of the hot dog. It was lukewarm and felt like a rock in my stomach, but if I didn't eat now, I would regret it later.

"What if it goes horribly wrong?" I finally responded. I peeked over at Shari, who was taking a swig of her soda. She used her knee to hold the steering wheel steady as she twisted the cap back on and placed the bottle into the cup holder.

"What would *'going horribly wrong'* look like?" She glanced over at me for a moment and then turned her focus back to the road.

I wiggled in my seat. All of this talk about Dave, all of this dredging up the past, made me feel as if my skin was tightening around me and there was nothing I could do about it. I'd left Tennessee with one purpose in mind—to put that life behind me. Now, I was entering back into the world I'd tried to forget, and my body was struggling to keep up with that idea.

"I don't know. He's married. He looks incredible. He lives in a mansion and has million-dollar music deals." I sighed as I looked out the window. "Anything that looks even remotely better than my current situation."

Shari's hand appeared in my peripheral vision. She snapped a few times, causing me to look over at her. She wasn't focused on me, but her lips were pursed, and I could tell that she wasn't happy with what I'd said.

"Dave doesn't have you, and he doesn't have Blake. Whatever life he's living right now pales in comparison to what you have. We forget that family is what is important.

Even if he has money and fame, when he's on his death bed, he's going to regret what he did to that little boy." There was so much emotional charge to her voice, that tears began to brim my eyelids.

I swallowed, hoping to push that reaction down deep, but all I did was swallow against the lump that had formed in my throat. She was right. No matter what kind of life Dave was living now, he didn't have Blake. He'd walked out on the best thing that he had ever created.

I needed to remember that. This whole trip was so I could create a better life for my son. Sure, Dave might have what he wanted right now, but I had what was important. And I was going to fight like hell to create a future that Blake would flourish in.

"You're right," I whispered as I swiped at the tear that had escaped. "He will always lose because he chose something other than his son."

Shari nodded. "That's right." She glanced over at me. "You're doing the right thing, and I'm here to help you remember that."

I smiled. The pit in my stomach hadn't disappeared but it had lessened. And I was grateful for Shari's insistence that this was important. I'm not sure I would have ever come to that conclusion myself. I might have thought about it, but I would have never put the actions into place to make it happen.

"Was it this hard for you and Craig?" I asked, cracking the lid to my soda and taking a sip. The fizz stung the inside of my mouth.

Shari was quiet for a moment. "It was. It was really hard. He broke me in a way that I hadn't realized."

My heart hurt for her, but there was a sort of camaraderie that came from two women having their lives turned upside down. We knew what the other was feeling without having to say the words. And that strengthened the bond between us.

Then a question formed in my mind. One that I wanted to ask out loud, but I wasn't sure if it was my place to do so. Shari had come out of the dark tunnel of leaving the person that was supposed to love you. The person you had children with and the one you sincerely thought you'd spend the rest of your life with. She had to know the answer to my question.

Feeling brave for a moment, I parted my lips and asked, "Does it get easier? The pain? Does it eventually lessen?"

Shari was quiet for a moment, and I worried that I'd asked the wrong thing. I wanted to take the words back, but she took in a deep sigh, and I could see her smile spread across her lips.

"It does. It's slow. Sometimes it feels like molasses coming out of a jar, but it does get easier. It's not all at once like I wished it would be. It took spending time with myself, spending time with my kids, and honestly, finding Danny to discover who I am now. I lived my life for Craig. I did everything for him. So when he was gone, I wasn't sure who Shari was anymore."

She paused as she changed lanes. Then she glanced over at me. "I worried that I was too broken for someone to love me. I worried that I would never be whole again." Her gaze drifted back to the road. The sun was starting to shift down the sky, its light casting shadows into the car. "But eventually you find your center of gravity. You start to realize that who you've been suppressing all this time isn't the enemy. The people who hurt you are."

I nodded, feeling as if she was saying exactly what I needed to hear. I'd pressed down my feelings for Dave and our breakup for so long that I wasn't sure who I was anymore. All I knew was that I didn't want to be broken Fiona anymore. I didn't want to hide behind fake smiles and hollow laughter. I wanted to be me. And I wanted to discover just who *I* was.

"Don't worry. You'll get there."

We sat in silence for a few minutes before Shari leaned forward and clicked on the radio. Soft music flowed into the car, and I found myself relaxing. This conversation definitely drained me but in a positive way. I was slowly letting out the murk that had built up inside of me. The part of me that held onto what had happened and didn't know how to let it go.

Even though I had a long way to go in this healing process, I was going to be okay because I'd taken the first step. I couldn't ignore my life with Dave any longer. Taking this trip was only going to strengthen me in the long run.

I was going to face my past and find a way to heal from it.

We didn't arrive in Nashville until one in the morning. The streets were humming with people even though it was a weeknight. I glanced around, watching the familiar places pass by me. So much time, so many memories were wrapped up in this place. Even though I'd only been gone for the better part of six months, a lot had changed. Or maybe I had changed.

We pulled into the parking lot of the hotel Shari had booked. We got out, stretching our arms high into the sky. My body ached from sitting in a cramped car, and I was ready to stretch out on a bed and fall asleep.

After checking in, we lugged our suitcases up to our room and crashed. I knew I should have been too nervous to fall asleep because of what tomorrow would bring, but I was too tired to worry. Tomorrow, I would face the music, but tonight, I was going to sleep in bliss.

We'd forgotten to close the blinds, and the sun woke us up early the next morning. I groaned and covered my eyes with my arm. Shari must have heard me because she mumbled, "Dumb sun," from the bed next to mine.

I pretended that the sun wasn't there for as long as I could before I sighed and sat up. I rubbed my eyes and pressed my hand against my lower back. I yawned as I glanced around the small but modest room we'd rented. It wasn't amazing, but after the trip we'd just taken, it was heaven.

I showered and got dressed. As soon as my brain registered what we were doing here, I couldn't lie around any longer. I needed to get up and get ready. I was going to need all my strength if I was going to face Dave today.

Shari was still tucked under her blankets when I

emerged from the bathroom, brushing my damp hair. I wandered over to the window and glanced down at the street in front of the hotel. People filled the sidewalks. Moms with kids wandered around, and people in business suits walked at a brisk pace as if they were late for something.

I studied them for a moment, methodically pulling my brush through my hair. It was strange how life went on around you like it did. No one was worried about Dave, or what he might say when I finally found him. I didn't exist to these people. They had no comprehension of my pain even though it felt so poignant to me.

"Sleep well?" Shari asked as she sat up in her bed. She rubbed her eyes and then focused her attention on me.

I nodded. "I guess so. At least, I slept as well as expected. You?"

Shari stretched her arms out in front of her and nodded. "Yeah. Despite the sun, I was out like a rock." She leaned back against her headboard. "I could have slept longer. It's nice when you don't have kids waking you up."

"Definitely."

I flipped through the travel brochures the hotel provided while Shari showered and got ready. After she was dressed, we headed downstairs for the complimentary breakfast. We called to check in with Danny who—despite looking disheveled—looked happy to see that we'd arrived safely.

I tried not to be envious of the affection I could hear in Shari's voice as she recounted the trip to him. I tried to ignore the look of utter attraction he had as she spoke. It made my heart ache that I had no one to look at me the same way.

Would I ever?

Thankfully, Blake decided that he wanted to see me, so I was able to push aside my feelings of pain and focus on my son. He was bouncing up and down on the couch, babbling on about what he and Danny had done the other day. I couldn't quite understand him through his excitement, but I tried as hard as I could. It was nice to see him, and I needed this turbo shot of energy he gave me if I was going to survive this trip.

I needed to remember who I was doing this for and that I had something amazing to come home to. No matter what happened here, I always had Blake. And nothing and no one was going to change that.

12

VICTORIA

I stood in my room at Mom and Dad's house, staring at the boxes that still needed to be filled. My clothes were scattered around the room. My dresser drawers were pulled out, still full of clothes. I was supposed to be out of here in two days, and right now, it looked like a war zone.

Thankfully, Mom and Dad were gone today. They were delivering a truckload of their items to the DC house, and Mom was determined to see that the items arrived safely. She forced Dad to tail the moving truck all the way down to their house, much to Dad's chagrin.

I didn't argue with Mom's choice though. It meant that I would have some time alone, and after my night with Brett, I needed some space to think.

"You can do this," I mumbled under my breath as I rolled up my sleeves. Thankfully, Maggie was understanding when I asked her for the day off today. She smiled, patted my arm, and asked if there was anything she could do to help.

I contemplated taking her up on that, but I knew she was busy at the inn, and I didn't want to inconvenience her in any way. So I just shook my head and gave her a smile.

Now, standing in front of the mountain of work that was packing up my room, I regretted not allowing her to help.

Breathing out a sigh, I pulled my hair up into a messy bun at the top of my head and pushed up my sleeves. I had this. I could handle this.

Just as I moved to fold the first shirt and lay it in a box, the doorbell rang. The chimes echoed down the large hallways and bounced into my room. Confused, I moved to my window that overlooked the front yard and strained to see who was here. But the front stoop was well concealed.

With no one else in the house, I made my way through my room and out to the hallway. It was probably someone delivering a package.

I pulled open the front door, ready to take something from a delivery person, only to stop dead in my tracks. Brett was standing on the other side of the door with a wide smile. When he saw me, his eyes lit up.

Strange.

"Wh-what are you doing here?" I asked, still not certain if I was actually seeing him or if I was hallucinating.

"I'm here to help."

"Help?" I glanced behind him toward the driveway. He

was alone, and there wasn't a kidnapper with a gun to his back. Was he here of his own volition?

He nodded and moved to step into the house. Out of habit, I backed away, so he could make his way into the foyer unabated.

"Yep. I'm here to help you pack. Mags said that you were stressed out and could use the help."

I took my time shutting the front door, so I could process what was happening. Brett was here. In my house. Looking determined. As if he could sense that I was going to resist but wasn't going to let me.

"Where's your room?" he asked as he kicked off his shoes.

My entire body heated from his question. Even though he meant nothing by it, my head instantly went there. Stupid, stupid head.

"Upstairs," I whispered as I waved toward the stairs.

His eyes followed my gesture, and before I could stop him, he headed in that direction.

I swallowed a few times, my mouth felt so dry. Then I glanced over to the entryway mirror and embarrassment rushed through me. I looked like a ghost, standing there with no makeup and my hair sticking out of my bun in every direction.

I peeked up the stairs to check that Brett wasn't looking. Then I quickly pulled my hair from the bun, smoothed it out, and pinched my cheeks for some color. I didn't really *care* about how I looked, but I did have an image to uphold.

Victoria Holt could not be seen as anything less than perfect.

By the time I got upstairs, Brett had already found my room. He was standing in the middle, surveying the boxes. When I entered the doorway, he glanced over at me.

"It's a good thing that I came. It's worse than I thought."

I moved closer to the very noticeable pile of underwear that I'd pulled out of a drawer and dumped on the floor. I stood in front of it, hoping to block it from view. "That's not fair. I've been trying," I said as I folded my arms and gave him a halfhearted pout.

Brett raised an eyebrow. "I find that hard to believe." Then he wandered over to my wall of bookshelves and tipped his head to the side as if reading the titles on the bindings. "You've got some interesting reads here," he said as he pulled out *Moby Dick*. "Some I would not have pegged you as a fan of." He slipped the book back into place and then glanced over at me.

I was midway through shoving my underwear into a nearby box. His stare startled me so much that I quickly stood, a lingering thong catching on my ring as I rose. I should have noticed the fabric tickling my fingers, but I didn't realize it was there until I glanced down to see the teal-green monstrosity hanging from my hand.

His gaze felt like a laser boring into me. I quickly tossed the thong into the box. I had half a mind to set fire to the whole thing and just buy new underwear. Every time I saw those pieces, I was going to remember this moment. I was going to remember him.

Thankfully, Brett didn't say anything. Instead, he walked over to my bathroom and looked inside. "So it's just this room?" he asked.

I nodded and then motioned down the right side of the hallway. "And my office. My bedroom and my office."

He glanced toward the doorway and then back to me. "All of this is not going to fit into your tiny room at the inn. Do you have a place for it?"

My sudden drop in expression tipped him off. He quirked an eyebrow before he chuckled and pulled out his phone. "I have a friend across the bridge who owns a storage place. Let me call him to see if he has an opening."

Relief flooded my body as I watched him bring the phone to his cheek and start to speak. I don't know how I forgot to schedule something like that. I wasn't normally this airheaded. I blamed it on the fact that Mom and Dad's announcement had caught me off guard, and I was trying to figure out the rest of my life in a matter of days.

I was completely out of my element.

It didn't take long before Brett had secured me a spot. He hung up his phone and gave me a huge smile. "It's done." Then he nodded toward the room. "Let's get this place packed up."

I assigned Brett to work on the bookshelf while I tackled the dresser. There was no reason to relive the underwear fiasco. I was so embarrassed that he'd seen it. I would probably light up in flames if he touched them.

Brett hummed softly while he worked. It was calming to listen to him. Heck, it was calming just to have him near me. I normally felt so alone in this house, but to have Brett here to help me—it was nice. It was something that I could get used to.

His humming was broken by a chuckle. I glanced over to see him with my high school year book. I realized what he must be looking at, and I ran over to him as fast as I could.

"Don't look at that," I said as I snatched the book from him.

He raised his hands, allowing me to tuck the book safely against my chest. I glowered at him, but his smile was so genuine that I was finding it hard to be mad at him.

"I'm sorry, I didn't think." He pushed his hands through his hair and then shrugged. "I wasn't laughing in a ha-ha funny way. I was laughing because you were adorable."

I blinked as my brain struggled to comprehend his words. "What?"

He shrugged. "I mean, you weren't the beautiful woman you are now, but you can see the potential there." He turned his attention back to the bookshelves.

"I'm sorry. What did you say?" It was as if my mind couldn't wrap itself around the conversation.

He glanced over his shoulder. "Which part didn't you understand?"

I cleared my throat, hoping that was all it was going to take to clear my mind. Nope. I still felt cloudy. "Everything. All of it."

He chuckled and turned. "You have to know that you are beautiful, Victoria."

My eyes stung with tears. My throat felt as if it were closing. No, I didn't know that. No man I'd ever been with—for the short time I was in a relationship—had ever said those words to me.

My silence must have tipped him off because, a moment later, he was turning to face me. His gaze swept over me, and I felt so raw and exposed in a way that I'd never felt before. And I was a woman who was used to giving speeches in front of crowds.

Add in my issues with my parents and I was a jumbled mess of emotions. Suddenly, Brett was across the room. He brought his fingers to my cheek and swiped at the tear that had rolled down. I sniffled as I allowed myself to lean into him.

I wanted to be loved. I wanted to depend on someone. And even though I was fighting it, there was a part of me that wanted that someone to be Brett.

Not sure what to do, I slowly brought my gaze up to meet Brett's. His brow was furrowed as he stared down at me. I hated and loved the unabashed way that he studied me. It was as if I was the only person he saw. As if I was all that mattered in this moment.

It was a strange sensation.

"I didn't mean to make you cry," he said. His voice was deep and rugged. It sent shivers down my back.

I shook my head. "I'm not crying because of that," I whispered.

His fingers made their way from my cheek to under my chin, where he gently tipped my face up, so I had to meet his gaze. There was no hiding how I felt anymore. He was going to see the fear that I held inside. He was going to know that I was scared.

"Then why are you crying?"

I swallowed as I held his gaze. I wanted to be strong, but I couldn't. Not when I felt so weak. "I don't know."

Brett studied me for a moment before he dropped his hand and took a step back. His smile was soft and inviting. Not at all like the cocky one he'd been sporting earlier. "I like you, Victoria. I've been trying to make that clear, but I've been failing miserably at it."

My ears rang at his admission. I stared at him, wondering if I'd heard him right.

"You do?"

Great. What a time for the English language to completely fail me.

Brett scoffed. "Yeah. You didn't pick up on that? With the flirting and the failure of a date last night?"

"That was a date?" I couldn't help but laugh at what he said.

He nodded. "Yeah. Hey, I never said I was suave."

I clasped my hands in front of me and pressed them down, rounding my shoulders to release the pressure that had built up in my muscles. It was strange, having Brett just come out and say it like he did. Was this normal? Or was he playing a joke on me? I'd never experienced this before.

He was watching me when I brought my attention back to him. He looked expectant. For a moment, it felt nice to have the power back. I'd felt so out of place around him that knowing how he felt calmed me.

All the worry and questioning were gone.

"What?" I asked, shrugging.

He scoffed as he stepped closer. "I'm standing here, baring my soul, and that's all you have to say? 'What?'"

I didn't fight him as he drew near. Instead, I found myself leaning toward him. It didn't take long before he was inches away from me. Even though he wasn't touching me, I was acutely aware of the space between our bodies.

"Normally, this is where the dame tells the bloke how she's been in love with him all this time as well." His hand found its way to my hip, but I didn't pull away. My hands rested on his chest, and I could feel his heartbeat and the warmth of his skin through his thin t-shirt.

"Dame and bloke?" I asked, narrowing my eyes as I tipped my face up. Our lips were inches away now. All he had to do was dip down, and all of this anticipation would come to fruition.

He shrugged. "What can I say, old-timey movies are a guilty pleasure of mine." He leaned in even closer. "So? What do you say?"

I tipped my lips up into a smile. "About you watching old-timey movies? It's cute but a little nerdy," I said as I bit my lower lip.

He growled, tightening his grip on my hips. My hands slipped up to his shoulders in response.

"About what I just confessed to you."

I could hear the desperation in his voice. He was like

me. He wasn't a vulnerable type of person. The fact that he'd confessed liking me felt like an oddity for him. Knowing what it felt like to be vulnerable, I pulled back slightly so I could meet his gaze.

I wanted him to understand that this was hard for me as well. "I like you, too," I whispered.

That was all it took to unleash something in Brett. Suddenly, he crushed his lips to mine. His arms wrapped around my waist, pressing my stomach against his. All thought left my mind as I allowed his kiss to overtake me.

I hadn't realized until now how much I needed this. How much I'd missed physical touch. I'd convinced myself that I was okay. That I could survive on my own.

Not anymore.

The feeling of Brett next to me. The feeling of his hands pressed into my waist. His lips exploring mine. All of it filled the hole inside of me that had existed for too long.

Brett pulled back and glanced down at me. His hand was tangled in my hair, and there was a need in his gaze that took my breath away. I quietly groaned, wanting him to come back to me. It was as if I could kiss him forever.

He chuckled. "I really did come here to help you pack your room."

I glanced up at him, my eyelids heavy. It was as if my entire body responded to Brett and longed for him to hold me against him once more. "I know," I whispered as I drew circles around his chest.

He twitched, and I reveled in the fact that I could cause a reaction like this in him. It made me wonder what else I could do to cause a reaction. Suddenly, his hand was engulfing mine as he held it still for a moment. When I glanced up at him, he had a pained expression on his face.

"Did I hurt you?" I asked, worried that I'd taken this whole thing too far.

Brett just tightened his arm around my waist as he closed his eyes. A few seconds ticked by before he took in a breath and glanced down at me. "No. Not pain. Just..." He reached up and tucked some hair behind my ear. "Let's focus on something other than each other." He leaned forward and pressed his lips to my neck. "Before I lose my control."

I raised my eyebrows at his words. The desire to be closer to him rose up inside of me. But he was right. We were here for a job, and we needed to finish it. I was ready to pack up my belongings and get out from under my parents' heel.

Even though we didn't want to separate, we eventually made our way back over to the parts of the room that we were packing. We fell into a rhythm. Every so often, we glanced to the other and smiled. The room felt calmer, and even though I was packing up my life and moving, I felt hopeful.

For the first time in a long time, I was discovering who Victoria was.

And I kind of liked her.

13

FIONA

My feet hurt. My back hurt. My soul hurt.

We'd spent the better part of the day scouring my old stomping grounds, searching for Dave.

It was safe to say that Dave wasn't doing better than me. None of the local bars that had any clout had heard of Dave much less remembered if they'd seen him. That meant he'd either moved or wasn't performing anymore. I wasn't sure which I was frustrated about more.

After all, he'd told me that making music was his destiny. It was what he was born to do, and he would do it no matter what. It was this obsession that caused me to wake up and realize that I needed to leave with Blake. I'd needed to move on because I couldn't see a future with Dave.

When I finally caught up with him, we were going to have words.

"You hungry?" Shari asked, pulling me from my thoughts. I turned to see that she'd paused in front of a small Italian restaurant and was studying the menu. The smell of marinara sauce and garlic bread caused my mouth to water.

"Yeah. I could use the break."

She gave me a grateful smile. "Same."

I stepped up to the front door, and Shari followed behind me as I stepped inside. It was a small shop—it reminded me of the coffee shop at home. A woman was standing behind the small hostess stand. She was swiping a card through her credit card machine when she looked up.

"Just a minute, ladies."

Shari and I both nodded as we lingered by the door. A few guests passed by us as we waited. It wasn't long before the hostess looked up and gave us a smile. "Just the two of you?"

"Yep."

She grabbed two menus and waved for us to follow her. We were seated at a small table in the back. Once she handed over the menus, she took our drink orders and left.

I sighed, my feet relaxing now that I wasn't on them. Walking all over town was exhausting.

"I didn't realize how much I needed this," Shari said after taking a big gulp of her water.

I nodded. "Me too."

A silence fell over our table. I could tell that Shari wanted to ask me something, but I wasn't sure if I wanted to know what that was. I honestly didn't want to know if she felt helpless about our situation. We'd come all the way here, and I was going to feel guilty if we left empty-handed. After all, this was my idea and my ex. I had to take some responsibility for it failing.

"How are you feeling?" Shari finally asked just as our waiter dropped off a basket full of bread. We ordered, and the waiter left, leaving me to chew on her question.

I sighed as I picked at the crust of the slice of bread I'd picked up. "I don't know. Not good. I feel as if we are going to leave with nothing accomplished."

Shari's lips tipped up into a smile. "Then we keep looking. I'm sure we'll find Dave somewhere. I mean, this is Nashville. I bet we've only scraped the surface of the places he could be."

I nodded. That was very true.

"Fiona?"

A soft, melodious voice caused me to look over my shoulder. Yasmine was standing behind me next to a large man. Her eyebrows were raised as she swept her gaze over me. "I thought that was you," she said as I pushed out my chair and stood.

"Yasmine?" I asked as we embraced. "It's been so long."

We pulled apart and she nodded. "Yeah. It has."

I glanced between her and Shari. "This is my neighbor from when I lived here. She has the best singing voice ever."

Shari smiled and waved.

"This is Shari, my friend."

Yasmine waved back before she turned to focus on me.

"What are you doing here? And where is Blake?" She glanced behind me as if she were looking for him.

"He's back in Magnolia." Then I sucked in my breath as Yasmine focused her attention back on me. "I'm looking for Dave. There's no way that you know where he is, is there?"

She smiled as she worked the gum in her mouth. "Dave? Oh yeah, I know where he is. He's playing at the same club I am tonight." Then she furrowed her brow. "Are you wanting to get back together with him?"

I shook my head. "Oh no. Nothing like that." Then I leaned in. "I'm trying to find him for Blake."

Yasmine's face softened like it always did when it came to my son. She'd been there for me in the early months of Blake's life. She'd watched him so I could nap and bought him the most ridiculously loud presents. "Stop by the Laughing Cow tonight, and I'm sure you'll catch him. He plays early—that's the only slot he could get."

I nodded. "What time?"

She glanced behind her to the beefy man. "Five? Five thirty?"

The man nodded, and Yasmine turned back to me. "Make it five and you're sure not to miss him."

I hugged her again. "Thanks so much. This helps us out a lot."

Yasmine chuckled. "Of course. Anything I can do to help my bestie." She gave me a tight squeeze. "Don't be a stranger. And bring that baby next time. We may be friends, but he's my godson. I want to see him."

I laughed as I pulled back. "Will do."

The waiter brought us our food, so we said our goodbyes and Yasmine left. I glanced over at Shari, who looked as if she had a sudden surge of energy.

"This is good, right?" I asked as I spun my pasta around on my fork and then slipped the food into my mouth.

"If it saves me from running all around town, then it's great."

I nodded in agreement. We finished our food with renewed vigor. After we paid and left the restaurant, I found that I had a new spring in my step even if I was dreading what the night would bring. I'd found Dave and was going to have a conversation with him. I was confident that he would agree to start helping with Blake, and then I could help out Mom while I discovered what I really wanted to do with my life.

I was starting to see the light at the end of the tunnel and it was bright. The darkness of my time as a single mother on my own was going to come to a close. Mom would be happy, Blake would be taken care of, and my life would finally be able to start.

I was sure there were still stumbling blocks in front of me, but I was hopeful. And it was that hope that I was going to cling to.

―――

The club was pretty empty when we walked in at five. After spending some time in the hotel—even napping for a bit—we got ready. I knew Shari was worried about me. She kept looking at me with a worried gaze before she focused her attention on freshening up her makeup.

After what felt like the millionth look, I sighed and gave her a smile. "I'm okay. I really am. We'll be fine." I patted her shoulder. "I'm optimistic that Dave will be reasonable and that things will turn out the way they need to."

Shari's shoulders relaxed as she nodded. "That makes me happy to hear. And if it doesn't happen that way, I'm here to lay down the law."

I chuckled as we slipped on our shoes and shouldered our purses. "Good to know."

Now that I was standing in the club with a few other guests milling around me, staring up at the stage, some of that confidence had waned. Well, not some—all of it. My palms were sweaty, and I felt light-headed. I recognized Dave's guitar on the stand next to the microphone, which meant he was here. And it was only a matter of time before I was going to come face to face with him.

"Here," Shari said, shoving a beer in my hand. "It'll take the edge off."

I nodded as I took a sip. The taste only made my stomach ache, but I pushed through. I was a mess, and if I was going to survive the night, I needed a confidence booster. "Cut me off at two, or I'll get too tipsy to speak," I mumbled as I pointed to the bottle.

Shari was taking a drink of her seltzer, so she just gave me a quick salute.

We found a small table in the corner. Thankfully, there

were still some open places as the crowd began to fill in. If I was going to last the night, I needed to be sitting.

Just as five thirty rolled around, the lights dimmed, and Dave made his way to the microphone followed by a few guys I didn't recognize. He must have ditched the band members that used to follow him around when we were together.

Seeing the change in him—the length of his unkempt hair, the darkness of his gaze as he scanned the audience—caused my stomach to churn. My optimism was replaced with dread. Was this a good thing? Should I be here?

What if he demanded that he see Blake on a regular basis? Was I going to be able to let my son go with his father, whom I wasn't sure if I could trust?

I swallowed against the lump in my throat. I couldn't think like that. Dave was never a bad guy. He was just someone who had his priorities misplaced. My senses were just heightened from stress. I was certain that all I needed to do was speak to him, and things would work out in both our favor.

They had to.

The music started up, and I found myself bouncing my foot to the beat. He'd gotten better, that was for sure. His voice wailed into the microphone, and familiar lyrics met my ears. I remembered this song even if he'd changed the music that went with it. It was a song that he wrote for me.

It was strange to hear it again.

The set lasted for a half an hour before he introduced the next band. Once he was done, he hurried to gather his guitar and left the stage. Not sure where he was going to go from here, I stood.

"Oh, we're following?" Shari asked. She'd been happily munching on some nachos she'd ordered.

"Yep. I doubt he'll come around, and we want to intercept him before he leaves." I shouldered my purse and headed toward the door that I was fairly certain led to the backstage hallways.

Thankfully, no one was guarding that door. This wasn't the most expensive place, so the performers didn't need the protection that well-known artists needed.

I pulled open the door, and the flood of fluorescent lighting made me squint. Shari hurried behind me as we made our way into the empty hallway. It didn't take me long to find Dave's dressing room. I could hear his voice carrying from the other side.

I took a deep breath as I stared at the door. This was it. This was the first time I was going to confront my ex in months. Even though I'd left amicably, I was fairly certain that he was not going to be too happy with me showing up out of the blue and demanding money from him.

"All right, all right, I'll grab you a drink." The door suddenly opened and standing in front of me was Dave. His hair was pulled back into a bun at the top of his head, and he looked more upbeat. As if the man I saw on stage had disappeared.

"Fiona?" Dave took a step back. "What are you doing here?"

The bassist stepped up next to Dave and slung his arm

across his shoulders. "Who's this?" he asked, nodding in my direction.

The tone of his voice sent a shudder down my spine. I didn't like the way he was leering at me. Dave glanced over at him and then tossed the bassist's arm from his shoulders. "Get off me," he said before he shot me an apologetic smile. "This is the ex I've talked about."

"Alisha?"

"Fiona," Dave hurried to say.

I furrowed my brow. He'd dated my ex-friend, Alisha? Figures.

"And you're her...sexy older sister?" The bassist motioned toward Shari.

Shari laughed. Not in a *you're so funny* kind of way. But in a *har har* way. "I'm her friend, Shari. And I'm not interested." She nodded toward him before giving me a look that said, "Are you serious?"

I gave her a sheepish look before I turned my focus back to Dave. He was studying me. I took a deep breath. It was now or never. "I need to talk to you. Can we go somewhere private?"

Dave raised his eyebrows. Then he glanced over at the bassist, who was still smiling a bit too wide in Shari's direction.

"What about you?" the bassist asked, pointing his finger toward Shari. "Want to go somewhere private as well?"

Shari laughed and then turned, leaning into me. "I'm going to go see if my nachos are still there. If you need me, text."

I nodded. I was actually grateful she was giving me some space. I needed to deal with Dave on my own. I knew that Shari had the best of intentions, but I wasn't sure if she would be able to help me in the way I needed. "I will."

She gave my arm a squeeze before she disappeared back into the club.

Now Shari-less, I turned to Dave. For the first time, I noticed that he had a wad of bills in his hand. "Are you going to get something?" I asked, motioning toward the money.

He turned it around in his hand. "Yeah. I was going to grab us drinks."

"Perfect. I'll go with you," I said as I stepped to the side and waved for him to lead the way.

He paused before turning back to the bassist and then nodded. "Okay. I guess that'll work."

The dressing room door shut behind him as soon as he stepped out into the hallway, and we were suddenly very alone. I cleared my throat as I nodded at him, not sure what I was supposed to say or do. Did I just jump into the conversation? How was I supposed to prep him for this?

"I guess we'll just head out to the bar."

"Okay," I said as I stepped up next to him.

We walked in silence until we got to the door. Dave paused, turning to face me. "Is Blake okay?" There was a concerned hint to his voice that made me realize that not telling him why I was here could be problematic.

"Oh my gosh, yes," I said as I fished my phone from my

back pocket. "He's gotten so big." I swiped it on and showed him the picture of Blake that I had as my wallpaper.

Dave studied it for a moment before he nodded. "He has gotten big."

I turned the phone screen back to me and nodded. "He really has. And he's gotten stubborn."

Dave chuckled. "Something he got from his mom."

I shrugged as I clicked my phone off and slipped it back into my pocket. "I can't fight that statement."

Dave leaned his shoulder against the nearby wall and studied me. "So if Blake's okay, why are you here?"

Oh, we were going to do this now. I hadn't expected that, but since he asked, this might be the only segue I was going to get. I cleared my throat, straightened my posture, and put my best lawyer face on. I wanted him to know that I was serious about what I was about to ask.

I took in a breath and spoke. "I think you need to start paying child support."

The words hung in the air as Dave's expression froze. It was as if time stood still. Then a moment later, his expression dropped, and he reached out and pulled open the door. The music from the band that was performing carried into the empty hallway.

Just when I thought he was going to sprint through the club to get away from me, he turned and with a serious expression said, "No."

He turned on his heel and headed out into the club with the door slowly closing behind him.

I was left standing in the hallway, alone.

All of my fears. All of my insecurities boiled to the surface. What I had thought was going to be easy had been flipped on its head, and suddenly, I had no idea what I was going to do. If Dave didn't want to help out, what other options did I have?

And just how hard was this going to be?

A dark cloud began to settle around me, and I felt myself slip into the uncertainty that was my future. I allowed it to linger for a moment before I steeled my gaze and steadied my resolve.

I was here for my son and our future. And despite feeling like Dave had just slapped me in the face, I wasn't going to let him win this one.

I was going to stand up for myself.

If he thought he could get rid of me this easily, then he had another thing coming to him.

I wasn't done.

Not by a long shot.

14

VICTORIA

Brett and I finished packing my room in record time. It helped that we remained on opposite sides of the room at all times. Every time he even attempted to get close to me, I scolded him with a finger waggle and sent him back over to focus on his side.

I knew the moment I let him cross over that imaginary line, I was going to lose all will to pack. I wasn't going to be able to banish him to the corner, and we would focus on a lot more than just packing.

And with a two-day deadline looming over me, there wasn't time to play around. This was my opportunity to get my life in order. Mom and Dad were going to be back tomorrow, and the last thing I wanted to do was hang out here with their judgmental sighs and passive-aggressive sideways glances.

So as much as I wanted to explore my and Brett's new

relationship, this wasn't the time. I had to pull out professional Victoria to keep us in line.

Brett was hanging out on my stripped mattress when I wandered in with the vacuum cleaner. After plugging it in and working on the corner, I could feel Brett's gaze on me. My cheeks heated as I tried to ignore him, but it was hard not to peek over in his direction.

What was he thinking? Was he regretting our kiss? Did he want to take it back?

I inwardly shushed my worries. I was being ridiculous. He was the one to confess first, and I needed to start learning to trust. Half a day had gone by, and I was already starting to doubt what he said? If I was going to allow myself to linger on those thoughts, I might as well check myself into a mental institution 'cause I had problems.

Two warm, strong arms wrapped around me as Brett slipped his hand down my arm and grabbed hold of my hand, so we were holding the vacuum together. Warmth rushed across my skin at every point of contact. I inhaled sharply, my body responding to his closeness.

"What are you doing?" I asked as I clicked off the vacuum and half turned to look at him.

He glanced down at me, his half smile lighting a fire in my stomach. "You're really sexy when you vacuum." He wiggled his eyebrows.

I was sticky with sweat and fairly sure that my hair was sticking every which way. I knew he was being sweet, but he was outright lying.

"I think you're blind," I said as I turned to focus back on

the vacuum. I clicked the power back on and began moving across the floor once more.

Brett didn't step away. He moved along with me as if I needed his help to complete this task. I didn't, but I enjoyed how close he was to me. For the first time in a long time, I wasn't alone. It was a strange and exciting, albeit terrifying, experience.

It took a lot for me to trust someone, and as much as I wanted to trust Brett, it still didn't come easily.

After I finished vacuuming what I could—we'd stacked the full boxes along one wall—I turned the vacuum off. Brett stepped away from me and leaned against the wall as I wrapped up the cord and pushed the vacuum over to the corner of the room. Then I dusted my hands off and let out a sigh.

My whole life was about to change. Everything that I'd grown accustomed to was disappearing, and I was going to be on my own with no parachute. It was strange and liberating at the same time. I liked this amount of freedom but feared it as well. It was a strange mix of emotions that left me feeling confused and hollow.

"You okay?" Brett asked. He stepped closer to me, but I wasn't sure I wanted to be touched in this moment.

I was working through something, and even though I was sure Brett could be a great sounding board for me to do that with, I wasn't sure I had the energy to hash it out right now. "I need a shower" —my stomach growled— "and some food."

He nodded. "I'll get my guys over here tomorrow, and

we can get the boxes moved. For now, let's head back to the inn and get cleaned up. I was thinking we could head across the bridge for some dinner and celebratory drinks."

I wasn't in the mood for a big party, but a night out with Brett did sound amazing. I could let my hair down and just be me. It was the perfect way to send off my old life and usher in my new one.

I followed behind Brett as we drove to the inn. Once we got inside, he graciously let me take the first shower, which I thanked him for with a featherlight kiss. He didn't push me for more, which I appreciated. Any guy that I'd dated in the past always went for the kiss and a grab. But not Brett. He was gentlemanly as he stepped aside and waved toward the shower.

"See you on the other side," he said as I shut the door behind me.

The hot water and steam had a healing effect on me. I stood under it for longer than I should have, but by the time I got out, smelling like my strawberry and cream body wash, I felt better. A lot better.

I gave Brett's bathroom door a *shave and a haircut* knock and then hurried to my room as I was wrapped only in my towel. Brett opened his door just as I shut mine. Our gazes locked, and my cheeks heated as deep, raw desire flashed in Brett's eyes.

Not wanting to dive into what that meant, or even allow myself to linger on it, I gave him a soft smile and shut my door, locking it with a resounding click. I let out my breath, knowing what I wanted but not wanting to allow myself to think those things. Diving too fast into a relationship had been a problem in my past. I was determined to take things slow with Brett—feel things out.

I couldn't get too attached to a man who would most likely grow tired of me and leave.

Pushing all thoughts of Brett aside, I moved to dress in a floral top with jeans, and then I stood in front of the vanity mirror, towel-drying my hair. I allowed my thoughts to get lost in the monotony of sliding the towel from my roots to the ends. For the moment, I wasn't going to think. I wasn't going to decide what my future held.

For the first time, I was just going to allow whatever came to come.

I left my hair to air dry as I put on my makeup. Then I finished with the blow-dryer. After I calmed the flyaways, I slipped on my shoes and knocked on the bathroom door. When Brett didn't respond, I opened it and glanced inside.

He wasn't there, which meant he was most likely getting ready in his room. I knocked on his bathroom door, and a second later, it opened. A damp-haired Brett with an open button-down shirt greeted me. Instantly, my gaze went to his chest. He wasn't a ripped guy by any means, but he was muscular, so much so that my jaw dropped a bit.

Not wanting to be caught staring at his chest, I cleared my throat and forced my gaze upwards to meet his. He was smiling as he started buttoning his shirt.

"Geez, Victoria. Make a guy feel exposed," he said as he moved away from the door and back into his room.

I blinked, forcing words to form in my mind so I could

speak a cohesive sentence back at him. There was no way I was going to allow him to have the last word. "You could have waited until your shirt was on *before* you opened your door."

Brett sat down on his bed, his shoes sitting next to him on the floor. "Yeah, but then I would have missed your shocked expression." He gave me a wink before he bent down and picked up one of the shoes. "That's an image I'm going to lock away forever."

I glowered at him—that was all the response I could muster—as I moved over to the small armchair in the corner next to the window and sat down. I waited while he finished dressing and grabbed his wallet and keys, slipping them into his pockets. "Are you ready?"

I glanced over and then nodded. "Yeah." I stood and made my way over to him. Just as I passed by, his hand brushed my arm as he reached down to entwine his fingers with mine.

That stopped me in my tracks, and I glanced over to see his soft expression as he studied me. "I'm excited for our first date," he said softly.

Date. That was a strange word to hear. It was one I'd definitely not heard directed at me in a long time. Not wanting him to see my insecurity or fear, I just nodded.

"Me too," I whispered.

Brett squeezed my hand and then led me from his room. Just as we cleared the doorway, we both stopped. Maggie was standing in front of the door holding a pile of folded towels with a shocked but smug look on her face.

"What are you two doing?" she asked, the tenor of her voice revealing exactly what she thought we were doing.

Brett chuckled. "Ever the matchmaker, Maggie," he said as he pushed his hand through his hair. "Despite what this looks like, it's an innocent relationship." He squeezed my hand.

I wasn't sure why Maggie seeing us bothered me so much. I wished I could just brush it off as nothing. After all, she already knew that I liked Brett, so why did a hollow pit form in my stomach at the way she was grinning. She looked like she'd won the lottery or something.

I wanted to correct her. Tell her that even though we'd kissed and were currently holding hands, that didn't mean that we were destined to be together. Brett wasn't Archer. For all I knew, this was as far as we were going to get.

Brett didn't know me. He didn't know the true me. Sure, I seemed exciting, but eventually he was going to learn that there was nothing but a shell of a person underneath what I played off as strength. I was broken, and I wasn't sure that Brett was the guy to help me feel whole.

I needed to get out from under Maggie's gaze, so I held tight to Brett's hand and began pulling him down the hallway. I was ready to get off the island and over to a town where fewer people knew who I was or why it was laughable that a man might show interest in me.

I was Victoria Holt. And for a moment in my room, I'd deluded myself into thinking that I could have a relationship with this man. Or at least, that he could actually like me. But the farther we got away from that moment we'd shared, the faster and harder reality had set in.

I gave us a ninety-ten chance of having a long-term relationship. Ninety being the chance that we would break up. Ten being the chance that, someday, a friend of ours would find Brett in the hallway, carrying a ring for me just like I had found Archer.

With those odds, I wasn't going to hold my breath that this was going to last.

Thankfully, the restaurant that Brett chose to take me to was small and quiet. The dining room only held a few dozen people, which meant there was no chance I was going to run into anyone I knew. Once we were seated, the waitress took our drink order. I ordered a glass of wine while Brett ordered a Coke.

When she left, Brett's focus was on me. Not sure where to look, I studied the menu. I didn't like the way he was looking at me. It was as if he knew something was wrong but wasn't sure how to ask. If I were honest with myself, I wasn't sure how I was going to answer him.

"You okay?" he asked after the waitress brought us our drinks and took our food order.

I nodded as I sipped my wine. "Yeah. I'm fine." I let out a sigh as I set my glass down on the table. "I'm just tired, you know. It's been a long, emotional week." I rested my elbows on the table as I rubbed my temples. "I'm just ready for it to be over and for my life to officially start."

"It was that bad?" Brett asked as he picked up a roll from

the basket on the table between us. He ripped it open and spread some butter on each side.

"Living at my parents' house?" I chuckled. That was a side of me I hoped no one would see. The Holt family was intense. "If you only knew."

Brett leaned forward after setting his roll on his plate and grabbed ahold of my hand. His thumb stroked my fingers, and even though he was being sweet, I wanted to pull away. Talking about my family riled me up. I wasn't used to the emotional turmoil that came when thinking about my family contrasted against the warmth that was emanating from where our hands were touching.

The heat and chill inside of me made my stomach churn. I wanted to pull away from Brett. I wanted to run away. All the feeling I'd had before was gone, and the thing that replaced it was fear. And that fear was wrapping around me like a snake wanting to squeeze every last ounce of life from me.

I was terrified.

Thankfully, our food was delivered, which meant Brett needed to return his hand to his side of the table. Once I got food in my stomach, the pain there began to lessen. The warmth of the mashed potatoes and steak had a calming effect on me, and I began to feel as if I could breathe.

My anxiety decreased as I studied Brett. We'd spent so much of the day talking about me, that we hadn't touched on his life. Sure, we'd shared an impulsive kiss in my room, but on a deeper level, I really didn't know him.

"Tell me about your family. Tell me about growing up." I raised my fork and pointed it in Brett's direction.

He was taking a bite of his fettuccine Alfredo with steak, so he finished chewing before answering. After he washed it down with his soda, he focused his attention on me. "My family? Me as a kid?"

I nodded as I cut a piece of steak and slipped it in my mouth. "You know about me and my crazy family, but I know nothing about you—except that you were a lawyer."

He leaned back in his chair, one hand resting on his thigh, the other hand resting on the table next to his plate. "There's not much to tell. I had a normal childhood. I have a sister and a brother that live in Arizona and California. We don't really see each other a whole lot." He cleared his throat as he moved to wipe his lips with his napkin. "My parents…" His voice drifted off as a sad look passed over his face.

From the pain in his gaze, I suddenly realized what I'd done.

"Oh my gosh, I'm so sorry. You don't have to—"

Brett raised his hand. "It's okay. I don't talk about the accident much, so it's always hard when I dust it off and face it again." He offered me a soft smile which made me feel a tad better, but I still felt guilty for the fact that I was forcing him to face this.

"That had to be hard," I whispered. I had a strained relationship with my parents, but that didn't mean that I wanted to lose them. As long as my parents were around, we had a chance to fix things. But once they were gone, that was a future we could never have.

I realized that before my parents left for DC, I needed to let them know that I still cared for them even if they'd hurt me.

"Enough about depressing things. Let's talk about your future. I know the inn is not where you want to stay, so where are you thinking you might settle down?"

Just like that, my stomach was in knots once more. So many unknowns filled my future, and I had no idea where I was going to land. Trying to figure it out while sitting across from Brett didn't make me feel settled. If anything, it made me feel antsy.

"Let's talk about something else," I said as I scooped up some mashed potatoes. "Like, where are we going to go after this?"

Brett shot me a confused look, but that only lasted for a moment before he nodded and began to rattle off a few places we could go for drinks. I settled back in my chair, listening to our options.

The one consolation from this dinner was the fact that I was finally full. After an entire day of packing, I'd needed some sustenance. But this dinner had also made me realize that no matter how I tried to frame my relationship with Brett, it felt as if I were coming to the same conclusion.

One that didn't end in my happily ever after.

15

FIONA

My ears still rang with Dave's last word. The one that I had feared to hear and yet wasn't surprised when he said it. It'd become the word most commonly used in our relationship before I left. When I wanted to go back to school. When I wanted to move to Magnolia. When I wanted him to spend more time with Blake and me instead of going out with his band.

That two-letter word had soured my stomach more than Blake vomiting all over me. That word tore at my confidence and made me feel like a child again.

No.

I blinked as I stared at the shut door in front of me. I wanted to run after him, grab onto his arm, turn him around, and demand that he talk to me. I deserved more than what he'd just said to me.

We'd been in love once. I had his child. We'd talked about getting married. Yet he still refused to man up and be the father that he needed to be for his son. To take care of him like he knew he needed to.

I felt lost and helpless.

And then, slowly, that helplessness turned to rage. A slow simmer that only took a few seconds to grow into a raging boil inside my gut. He wasn't going to do this to me. He wasn't going to do this to Blake. He needed to face the consequences of his decisions, and he needed to help take care of us.

Blake wasn't only my responsibility. Even if I wanted to pretend that I didn't need Dave, I knew that was a lie. I needed all the help I could get until my feet were under me. Then I could walk away, Dave could drop his child support, and we'd be fine. It was only until I was out of this ocean of despair that I was drowning in. I just needed the extra boost until I could arrive on solid ground.

I felt weak admitting that, but it was the truth, nonetheless. I needed Dave. Mom needed Dave. And Blake needed Dave. Our futures were inexplicably intertwined whether I wanted them to be or not. And I was going to stand tall and face whatever Dave was going to throw at me. I was tired of backing down. I wasn't going to do it this time.

Feeling confident, I squared my shoulders and pulled open the door. Music blared from the stage. I weaved between the club goers who packed the place. I had to pause a few times to squint through the dark room, but I finally located Dave and zeroed in on him.

Just as I neared the table he was standing at, a hand

grabbed my arm, halting my progression. I cursed and turned only to see the wide eyes of Shari as she stared at me.

"You okay?" she asked.

My jaw muscles were twitching I was so angry. The more I'd allowed myself to think about Dave, the angrier I became. I deserved better than this, and for the first time in my life, I was going to demand it.

"No," I said, sharply, and I turned and took a step toward Dave. Thankfully, Shari didn't push me further. She dropped her hand but kept close behind me. It helped having her there. It gave me the moral support that I didn't know I needed.

"Hey," I said as I grabbed Dave's arm and tugged. He'd been leaning on it as he talked to some midriff-showing girl with dark-blue hair and a belly button ring.

"What the—"

"He's a deadbeat father that will knock you up and then refuse to pay child support. If that's what you want your future to be, by all means, stick around." I ignored Dave as I glared at the girl he'd been hitting on. She gave me a dirty look as she grabbed her phone and drink and left me alone with Dave.

"What do you want, Fiona?" Dave spat as he turned to face me. There was a fire in his gaze that matched my own. He was angry with me, which only spurred my anger more.

"You can't just say no, Dave. That's not the way this works."

He chuckled as he downed the shot he had clutched in

his hand. He slammed the glass onto the table with a hollow thud. He took his sweet time to turn and square with me head-on. "What are you going to do?"

His height compared to mine was noticeable, and suddenly, I was having flashbacks of our relationship. He wasn't always the kindest man, but I'd always given him the benefit of the doubt. After all, I loved him, and he loved me. What did it matter if he was more particular about certain things than I was. Isn't that what love was? Compromise?

But now, standing in front of my past, I realized that I'd been wrong. There was nothing healthy about our relationship. There was nothing good about the way he treated me. He'd abused me. Not with his fists, but with his anger and his words.

"Hey, back off," Shari said as she moved to step between us.

Not wanting her to fight my battles for me, I gave her a soft smile as I pulled gently on her arm. The truth was, I needed to face my past if I was going to have any way of moving forward. If this was how Dave wanted to handle things, then he needed to realize that he was messing with the wrong woman.

Sure, I might not be in a good place financially. And I just might be ruining my mother's life by living with her, but I would find a way out of this eventually. I had to try.

"You're his father," I whispered. My throat tightened as the words slipped from my lips. How had I let this get out of hand? I was supposed to protect my son—do what was right for him. But right now, I couldn't pay for what he needed. I was failing him on the most basic level. I didn't like how it made me feel, but most of all, I didn't like that Dave didn't look as broken as I felt. It was as if he didn't even care.

"So you say," he snorted as he nodded toward the waitress who'd just dropped off another shot.

Those words stabbed me in the chest. Like daggers to my heart. "What's that supposed to mean?" I hissed.

He shrugged, all the while keeping his gaze locked on me as he downed his shot. "My friends talked once you left. I know you were sleeping around." He slammed the glass down on the table. "You say Blake's mine, but I never really believed it."

Acid rose up from my stomach. Was this why he didn't want to be listed on the birth certificate? He said being a single mom would look better for state assistance and that when he finally made it, he'd make his paternal status official.

I should have known.

"You're a snake," I growled as I stepped closer to him.

Dave didn't move. Instead, his hollow smile grew wider. "Looks to me like you're out of options. After all, how are you going to prove paternity? I'll never agree to the test. You've reached a dead end." He snickered as he pushed his hands through his hair. "Face it, Fiona. You're not going to lock me into this. My money is my money. I'm the one out here busting my ass to make it. You just tagged along for the ride, and now I'm kicking you off."

The tears clinging to my lids burned. I blinked, angry

that I'd allowed myself to even come down here. That I'd deluded myself into thinking this would be easy. How had I forgotten what it was like here? What Dave was like?

He was never going to agree to child support. He was selfish—always had been. I guess I wanted to believe that I hadn't been right about Dave. That there had been some good in him. Despite the fact that we'd broken up, I'd allowed myself to lie about who he was and what he'd put me through.

But standing right here, seeing it in his gaze, hearing his voice tell me once more that he didn't care for me like I cared for him—made the past that I'd walked away from all too real.

He'd been the bad guy. He'd always been the bad guy.

"I would watch what you are saying," Shari said, stepping in between us.

I could see that her hackles were up, and there was a tone in her voice that sent shivers down my spine. If I was in a fight, I wanted Shari in my corner. She was a strong woman. Stronger than I could ever be.

"Who are you?" Dave asked, his tone mocking.

He hated authority, and Shari had to appear that way to him.

"Your worst nightmare if you don't step up and take care of your family like a man."

Dave glanced over the top of Shari's head and met my gaze. "Seriously, who is this woman? I've met Anna, and this isn't her." Then he dropped his gaze back down to Shari.

"Are you the president of the quilting club back in Magnolia?"

I could tell Shari wanted to tell him more. She wasn't going to let him just walk out of the bar like this. She wanted him to pay. Maybe for me. Maybe for herself and what she went through with Craig. Regardless, she was a woman on a mission, and if I didn't pull her back now, I was going to lose this fight.

"Come on, Shari," I said as I linked arms with her. "It's not worth it." Then I glared at Dave. "You're not worth it."

Dave dropped his expression and hunched over. He gave us a mocking smile as he pretended to look hurt. "Oh no, hit me when I'm down," he said as his upper lip sneered at Shari.

She moved to approach him, but I just tightened my grip on her and began to guide her out of the club. This conversation was over. This vacation was over. What had started out as a nerve-racking but somewhat confident move on my part had now become my worst nightmare.

Once I walked away from Dave, I wasn't sure what I was going to do or who I was going to turn to. What sorts of rights did I have? If Dave wouldn't even agree to a paternity test, where was I going to go from here?

And how much would it cost me to get a judge to order him to take one?

Certainly more than I had in my bank account. And Mom wasn't going to be able to help. I'd opened this whole can of worms, so I could help her.

I was out of options and out of time. The last thing I

wanted was for Dave to see just what he was doing to me. I didn't want him to know that he'd won. I didn't want him to think that he could disown our son and get away with it.

Somehow, someway, he was going to pay. But if I showed weakness, I would crumble in on myself. And I couldn't do that. Not right now.

The sun had set behind the building when Shari and I stepped outside. Despite the encroaching darkness, the street was alive with tourists. The sounds and smells of the town rushed back to me, contrasting the experience that I'd just had.

A few hours ago, these same sights and smells had brought back what I thought were happy memories. But now that I was facing the truth of my past, these same memories just brought pain. I realized that I was not okay. That I'd never been okay. And I was as far away from being okay as I could possibly be.

"You alright?" Shari asked as she shouldered her purse and fell into step next to me.

I sighed and nodded, clinging to my own purse strap as if it were my lifeline. "I'll be okay." I offered her a weak smile.

She studied me, but I kept my gaze down. There was no way that I wanted her to see how defeated I felt. I didn't want her to regret helping me. After all, she'd seemed so enthusiastic when we first started our trip. How was I going to face her now?

The trip to our hotel was short, and as soon as we got into the room, I kicked off my shoes and collapsed on the bed. My entire body sank into the down comforter and soft pillows as I relaxed. I needed a minute to gather my strength before I could move.

"You're not okay, and that's fine. You shouldn't be okay. What that man did wasn't right. And he's going to pay."

I could tell that Shari was pacing the room, so I cracked my eyes open to watch her. Her forehead was wrinkled, and her eyes looked wild.

"But what can we do?" I asked as I pressed my hands into the bed and pushed up until I was sitting with my back against the headboard.

Shari stopped for a moment before she turned to face me. Then, slowly, a smile began to emerge. "I'm not 100% sure yet. I'll have to talk to Austin. But I think the first step is getting back to Magnolia and getting this" —she opened her purse and removed a shot glass from inside— "to a lab so they can run the DNA along with Blake's."

My heart began to pound as I slipped to the edge of the bed. I grabbed a nearby tissue and Shari placed the glass gingerly into my hand. Then she retrieved a plastic bag from her suitcase—apparently, she carried a stock of them with her to hold knickknacks that Bella picked up—and opened it. I slipped the glass inside, and she sealed it up.

"When did you take that?" I asked as I set it on the nightstand next to me.

She shrugged. "While he was being a donkey, I snuck it into my purse. I'm pretty sure it won't be admissible in court, but maybe it'll be the kind of proof you need to open a dialogue between you two."

I sat back down on the bed and brought my feet up, so I could hug my knees. I rested my chin on them as I nodded. I may be agreeing with her, but that didn't mean I had the kind of hope that she did.

I wish I had her optimism. It would be nice, thinking that some saliva off a glass and a lab would solve all my problems. It may have worked for Shari, but my situation was a little different.

Dave wasn't her ex, and my problems weren't her problems.

But Shari didn't seem to notice how helpless I felt. Instead, she patted my bed as she passed by, declaring that she was going to jump into the shower and then go to bed. We'd head out in the morning.

I nodded as I shifted to my side, propping the pillows up around me and staring at the wall. I was ready to go home. I was ready to see Blake. Even though Mom was going to want to know where I'd been, I was ready to see her.

Nashville was my past.

And I was ready to face my future even if it felt bleak. Even if it felt hopeless.

At least I had my son and my mom. And really, what else was there?

VICTORIA

The club was loud and grating on my nerves. I sat at the corner booth, trying hard not to think about what was sticking to me after I touched the top of the table. Whatever it was, the residue seemed to meld itself to my skin, and no matter how much I tried to wipe it off, it wouldn't budge.

My finger was permanently sticky.

Great.

Brett had left to grab us some drinks, which I was grateful for. I was ready to get this evening over with, so I could sit in silence and ponder my future. Which sounded more grandiose than it would end up being.

What would inevitably happen was me falling asleep on my bed with the TV going and half a bowl of ice cream on my lap. I would allow myself to think about what I was going to do with my future for about five minutes before it would overwhelm me, and I needed to escape until I felt better.

Sure, it wasn't healthy, but I was coping the best way I knew how. And that was all I could ask of myself.

Laughter by the bar drew my attention over. Ever since we walked into the club, every eye was on Brett. He certainly got around here and in Magnolia. All the women flirted with him, and all the guys gave him one-armed bro-hugs. It made me feel invisible, standing next to him and smiling awkwardly at people who weren't really interested in including me in their conversations.

I peeked around the booth to see Brett standing with a group of people. A blonde woman was standing close to him, tapping his arm as she laughed. Whatever he was saying had to be hilarious with the way she was going on. Or she'd never heard a joke before.

Whichever it was, she wasn't in a hurry to remove her hand or step away from him. A feeling of dread settled in my stomach, which overshadowed the feeling of jealousy that had started rising up. I was a mess of emotions, and I was struggling to figure out what I wanted for the rest of my life. But I was beginning to realize that dragging Brett along during this journey of self-realization wasn't kind to him or me.

He looked so relaxed in the choices he'd made. The way he smiled as he captivated the crowd made me realize that there was no way I was ever going to do that. I was never going to feel at peace with myself like that.

I was destined to be floundering forever.

Blowing my hair from my face, I settled back against the booth and sighed. What was I doing here? Why did I think this was a good idea? Why had I allowed Brett to talk me into all of this?

I was more than happy to sit back and wallow in my own self-pity. Live my life as a hermit where I growled at my neighbors and chased kids from my front yard. I was ready to be a recluse, and yet I'd allowed Brett to step into my life and change that for me.

He'd made me believe in myself. The only thing was, he didn't know who the true Victoria was. And I knew that once he discovered her, this would be over.

And I would be left alone and brokenhearted. And that thought was more than I could handle. It made me want to curl into a ball and die. I had the stress of my own happiness on my shoulders and adding Brett's felt like it would crush me.

And that made me ask, could I have that happiness? Was it even possible for me? I could never be like the blonde standing next to him, brushing his arm and laughing at what he said. I just didn't have that in me. It wasn't my personality.

I was always going to be the overly analytical person who questioned everything around me. I was always going to be the person who dragged around the drama from her overachieving parents who wanted her to perform the same way.

I was never going to be free of that.

And Brett deserved someone who could be as free as he was.

Tears stung my eyes as I blinked a few times. Was I seriously crying over this? I'd only just met this man. It would be ridiculous to think he was the one. Especially since I was fairly certain that *the one* didn't exist for me. He certainly wasn't this charismatic bartender who'd been dropped in my lap.

This was fate's cruel way of giving me a taste of what I wanted only to have it ripped from my grasp. The faster I walked away from Brett, the more I was going to save myself from the heartbreak that I knew was coming.

The heartbreak that I knew was going to crush me.

"Sorry that took so long." Brett's arm came into view as he set down my Diet Coke.

I'd drunk so much at dinner that I was ready for something that wasn't going to make my head spin, something that would give me the confidence I needed to walk away from what had brought me happiness during this dark moment in my life.

Brett deserved someone who had the sun rising on her future. Not someone stuck in the midnight portion of her life. I was only going to drag him down.

"You okay?"

I hadn't noticed that Brett was sitting across from me. I raised my gaze to see him leaning toward me with his brow furrowed. Not wanting to lose the little bit of control that I had, I forced a smile. This wasn't the time or place to break off whatever we had. I needed to put him off the scent if I was going to make it through the rest of this date.

"I'm fine." I took a sip of my soda and then shrugged. "Just tired."

Brett paused before he took a drink. He was watching me, and I could tell that he didn't believe me. But thankfully he didn't push me further. Instead, he sat back and glanced around the club before his gaze landed on me once more.

Needing to change the subject from the questions that were burning in his gaze, I glanced around, looking for something to direct his attention to. "You seem to have a lot of friends here."

When Brett didn't answer me right away, I peeked over at him to see that the furrow between his brows had deepened. He knew something was wrong, and it was becoming apparent that he wouldn't focus on anything else until we addressed what was going on.

And as much as I wanted to clear the air, I knew that the moment I told him how I felt, it would be the end of our date and the end of us.

"I'm actually really tired. Mind if we leave early?" I asked as I grabbed my purse and set it on my lap. Truth was, I was tired. It had been an emotional day, and I was ready to put it behind me. I was ready to crawl back into my cave and hide for the rest of my life.

Brett looked as if he understood before I even spoke. He slipped to the edge of the booth and stood. Then he extended his hand for me to grab. I studied it for a moment before I decided to take it.

We were friends after all. I could allow him to do nice things for me for now. I was going to set my boundaries later tonight. When we said goodbye, I would make sure that he knew where we stood. Where *I* stood.

But until then, I could still play the part of fun Victoria. Until reality hit, I would act like we were okay. I would enjoy the last few moments of happiness I had left.

The ride home was quiet. Brett turned the radio on, and a soft ballad flowed from the speakers and helped calm my ragged nerves. When we got to the inn, he pulled into the parking lot and turned off the engine. We sat in silence for a few moments. It was as if he sensed that something was going to happen and wanted to wait a bit more before having to face what our future inevitably held.

I glanced over at Brett as I took in a deep breath, my fingers playing with the door release on my right. I wanted to open the door, but I also knew that as soon as my feet hit the ground, we were going to be over. I needed to end whatever we were before I fell too hard.

He was staring straight ahead, his jaw working as if he were chewing on something. Did he know what I had planned? That I was going to end this?

"Is there something you need to talk to me about?" he asked and then paused before he glanced over at me. There was something in his gaze. Pain? Worry?

I wasn't sure how to interpret it or how I was going to react. As much as I wanted to put what he was feeling to rest, I knew that I couldn't lead him on. I couldn't make him believe that I was okay only to break up with him a few moments later.

I cared about him too much to do something like that.

"Brett," I said, his name coming out as more of a whisper than anything else.

He cleared his throat as he shifted on his seat. Then he glanced over at me once more as if preparing for what I was about to say. I felt like a bad person, breaking up with him like this. We'd only just started getting to know each other, and he seemed so happy. Doing this made me feel like crap. Only someone truly heartless would pull out the rug from the person they cared about.

But this was necessary. For me. For him. He deserved to be with the perky blondes of the world. Not me.

"You want to break up," he said.

His words caught me off guard, and I blinked a few times as I tried to register his words. He'd known that this was where I was headed? For a moment, I wondered if I was making a mistake. Did he really know me better than I realized?

Then I shook my head. That was ridiculous. After all, we'd only just met. How could he know me? *I* barely knew me.

"I'm sorry," I said, my voice sounding hoarse even though I'd barely spoken the whole night. My throat was tight with emotions to the point that I felt as if I were choking.

He shook his head. "No. It's okay. I get it." His hands tightened on the steering wheel as if he were strangling it.

"You do?" I asked.

He nodded. "Victoria, I want you to let me in. I want to show you what we could have. But if you don't want the same thing..." He sighed, his shoulders dropping as if they held more weight than he could handle.

And I felt for him. I wanted to reverse the last few days. I wanted to push him away from the start so that we didn't have to end up here. But pushing him away now was going to save heartache in the future. I'd rather struggle through a small amount of pain now instead of intense heartbreak later.

"I'm sorry," I whispered. And I meant it. This wasn't how I wanted things to start or end. I wished it could be different. I wished that I were different.

He nodded as he spun his keys around his finger a few times. "Yeah," he said as he turned to look at me. "Let's get inside. I'm tired."

We both pulled on the door release at the same time. We walked a few feet apart from each other as we crossed the parking lot and climbed the steps to the front porch. He held the door open for me, and I gave him a soft nod as I passed by.

Unfortunately, our rooms were off the same hallway, and we had to remain side by side as we walked toward it. That is, until we passed the dining room and stepped up to the door that led to the kitchen.

"Here's where we part," he said as he paused.

I stopped walking and turned to see that he was leaning

against the doorframe, his hands tucked into his front pockets.

"Oh, okay," I said, a feeling of sadness passing over me as I realized what this meant. We were done. We were parting for the night, but it was much more than that.

This was where we ended.

"Brett, I—"

He held up his hand. "You don't have to explain. I understand." He shrugged. "I don't like it, but I get why you are walking away."

I furrowed my brow. How did he know? Was he so confident he knew me that he could dissect my reasoning before I could? "I am…sorry," I whispered as if this was all it took to explain why I was acting this way.

He glanced down for what felt like an eternity before he looked back up at me. Then he sighed and shrugged. "I know. Someday, you'll discover what I see in you. Someday, you'll see that you are worthy of love and want to give it back." There was desire in his gaze, and it made me long for what he said to come true even if my head was only full of doubt.

I *wanted* to love him, and I *wanted* him to love me back. I wanted to allow myself to release the fear that had built up inside of me. But I was certain that would never happen. I was certain that wasn't in my future.

All I could do was offer him a small smile as some sort of lame consolation prize. I knew that he deserved better than what I could give him. I'd already pushed myself out of my comfort zone this far, and I doubted I could go farther.

"I'll see you around," he said as he pushed through the kitchen door and disappeared inside.

Now alone, I let out my breath. This day did not end the way I'd wanted it to. But it was an inevitable fate that I could see coming a mile away. I wasn't meant to find happiness. Not when I was such a failure at everything else in my life.

I pushed my hand through my hair as I made my way down the hall. After a long bath, I dressed in my comfiest pajamas and disappeared under my comforter. With a romantic comedy playing on the TV and a box of chocolates next to me, I wallowed in my self-pity.

If only I could be stronger. If only I could have more confidence, I might be able to find success in my romantic life. Before I met Brett, I was scared that there wasn't a man out there who would want to put up with my quirky personality and persnickety behaviors.

But then I met Brett and allowed myself to open up to the possibility of love. Now, after watching that relationship take a dive-bomb and fail, I had a whole new fear.

I was afraid that I would never be able to open myself up fully to love. That I would always be alone like I was right now.

And that thought scared me.

More than I thought possible.

FIONA

The ride back to Magnolia took less time than it took to get to Nashville. We were up bright and early the next day—before the sun was even up—and we rolled up to the coffee shop right before bedtime. I gathered my luggage from Shari's trunk, gave her a quick wave, and headed through the back door and up the stairs.

I could hear Mom singing as I stood outside of the door, gathering my strength to walk inside the apartment and fess up to what I had done. I didn't have to see her face to know that she wasn't going to be happy with me. I could imagine her disappointed sigh and the sadness in her gaze that happened every time I mentioned Dave.

My leaving home had broken her in a way that I hadn't realized until I came back. Until I saw the effect losing me had on her. It wasn't going to be easy to go in and tell her where I'd been the last few days, but I knew that it was the right thing to do.

Taking in a deep breath, I turned the door handle and pushed inside. Mom stopped singing and glanced up from where she was sitting. She had Blake's high chair pulled between her legs, and she was coaxing him to eat spaghetti. I dropped my bag on the floor and slipped off my shoes.

"Have a good trip?" she asked as she twirled the spaghetti around her fork and then brought it up for Blake to eat. He took the handle from her and shoved the food into his mouth.

"It was okay," I said as I made my way into the kitchen and stood next to Blake. I pushed his hair back away from his face. There were already streaks of sauce in it, and I wanted to mitigate the damage.

"Only okay? I thought you like the book club ladies."

I winced. I'd told her that we were going on an impromptu girls trip. Which had been somewhat accurate. After all, Shari was part of the book club, and the trip had been random. It was the destination that I knew Mom wasn't going to agree with.

"About that," I said after an internal battle with myself as I tried to decide if I should tell her. I couldn't keep this a secret forever—after all, I was in for a long legal battle. At least, that was what Austin had said when Shari called him during our drive back.

From the way Dave handled my request, I had little faith that involving the courts was going to motivate him to comply. Thankfully, Austin had some pro bono hours, which would greatly decrease the expense of hiring him.

And Shari may have guilted him a bit into taking me on.

With all of that going on, I knew that I was going to need as many people in my corner as possible. I needed Mom to support me—no matter what happened. And if I were honest with myself, I wanted her help. She might not be upfront with me about the coffee shop, but she cared about me. I knew that.

Mom raised her eyebrows as if to signify that she was listening. So I took a seat at the table as she continued to help Blake eat his food. But I could tell that her attention was on me.

"I went to Nashville," I said quietly.

Mom paused, her intrigued expression morphing to one of confusion. "Nashville? Why?"

I took in a deep breath, hoping that it would relax my muscles. It didn't. If anything, they felt tighter than ever.

"I went to find Dave."

Blake's fork clattered to the floor. I glanced down at it as Mom swore under her breath. She bent down and picked it up before she walked over to the sink to toss it in. I stood to help, but from the frustration on her face, I decided to stay out of her way.

Once she was sitting, I parted my lips to speak, but she raised her finger. "We'll continue this conversation after Blake is in bed."

I wanted to fight her. That wasn't how I wanted to handle this conversation. Blake was a safety cushion between us, and without him here, she wasn't going to hold back. I was going to feel her full wrath, and I wasn't looking forward to it.

It was torture, waiting in silence as we gave Blake a bath and then dressed him in his pajamas. There was a moment of released tension as I lay in bed with Blake and read him a book, but that was short-lived. Once we finished, I tucked him under his comforter and kissed him goodnight.

Dread filled my chest as I turned off the light and shut the bedroom door behind me. Now alone, I walked down the hall in search of Mom.

I found her sitting at the table drinking a wine cooler—a move she only made when she was stressed out. This was going to be a fun conversation.

I grabbed a soda from the fridge and sat down next to her. Might as well get it over with. There was no point in postponing the inevitable.

The crack of the soda tab broke through the deafening silence. After I took a drink and set the can down, Mom glanced over at me.

"Why did you go to Nashville? Are you and Dave getting back together?"

There was a break in her voice which surprised me. I studied her for a moment before I brushed it off and focused on her words.

"No. That wasn't why I went down there."

She blinked a few times as if she hadn't expected me to say that. Which made me feel somewhat excited. It was nice that I could still surprise my mother. Especially since I was fairly certain that she thought she knew everything about me.

She took a sip of her wine cooler and then turned her attention back to me. "Then why did you go down there?"

I took in a deep breath. Even though I wasn't prepared to have a conversation about what I'd seen and what that meant for our future, I knew that it was necessary. Especially if Mom and I were going to move past the past and focus on the future.

"I asked him to start paying child support. Or, at least, I wanted to arrange something with him."

Mom paled. A reaction I hadn't expected. She swallowed but looked as if she struggled with getting it to go down.

"You what?" she asked.

The temperature in the room began to rise. I could sense her agitation. I'd upset her, but I wasn't quite sure how.

"I saw the foreclosure notification. Things are bad, Mom. Your taking Blake and me in was a godsend, but I can't justify staying here at the expense of your house and business." I turned the soda can around on the table a few times before I swiped at one of the beads of sweat that had formed on the outside.

Mom was quiet as she stared hard at the tabletop in front of her. I wanted to read her emotions, but they were as foreign as the territory we'd just entered. Somehow, we were no longer mom and daughter, but the problem was, I couldn't quite tell what we were.

Eventually, I wanted to be friends, but that would be too much of a stretch in this moment.

"I'm not losing this place because of you," she whispered.

I leaned closer to her, not sure what she meant by that. "You're not?" I asked.

She shook her head. I could see that tears had formed in her eyes as she took a long drink of her cooler. Then she set the bottle down and slowly turned to me. "While you were gone, I was lonely." She shook her head and closed her eyes as if she were fighting what she was about to say. "I started going to the casino across the bridge. It was my mistake. I should have known better."

I stared at her. It was strange seeing my strong and resilient mother look so broken and downtrodden. How had this happened? My guilt for leaving only grew more intense. Had I pushed my mother to do this? Was it my fault?

Mom's hand enclosed mine and she squeezed it. "I didn't want you to know. I wanted you to think of me like I used to be. Before the addiction set in. Before I mortgaged this place." A tear slipped down her cheek. "Now I don't know what to do. But the last thing I wanted was for you to be involved. For you to think that this was somehow your fault." She gave my hand another squeeze. "This is my cross to bear, not yours."

I wanted to believe her. I wanted to think that, somehow, I had nothing to do with this. But I knew that wasn't true. I'd left her for a man who had never cared about me and who would continue to keep me at a distance. He broke my heart and pulverized it. And in my own way, I'd done the same to my mother.

"How do we fix this?" I whispered.

Mom's tired gaze met mine as she studied me. "I'm going to be honest, baby girl. I'm not sure." She leaned back and sighed. "I guess we start with being honest with each other. I don't want you leaving me again because I failed, but with the way things are going, I can't help but wonder if we will make it any longer here." She massaged her temples and then gave me a weak smile. "But if you're here with me, I'll be alright."

My heart swelled at her words. She may have been prickly with me when we first got here, but I was grateful that we were beginning to tear down the walls that we'd built up. Both of us had been trying to protect our hearts, but it was through leaning on each other that we were going to find the peace we were so desperate to obtain.

"Shari's brother is going to help me with all the legal stuff. We need to prove Dave's paternity, but after that, it shouldn't be too hard. I guess he's one of the best family lawyers around." I wanted Mom to have hope. This was my first step in helping out around here. Dave should help take care of Blake. Despite what he said, he was my son's father and he needed to honor his responsibility.

Mom's worry lines deepened as she studied me. "But what if Dave wants to take Blake away? I'm not sure I could handle losing him. He's what makes me get up in the morning."

That same thought had drifted through my mind numerous times as we drove back from Nashville. If I pushed this child support issue, was Dave going to push for visitation? As much as I didn't want my son to ever go off with his father, I forced myself to realize that Dave wasn't a bad guy. Sure, he was misguided, but if he wanted some time with Blake, I was going to try my hardest to honor it.

After all, Blake did deserve to know his dad. And I couldn't be the one to keep that relationship from growing.

But from the worried look on Mom's face, I knew my attempt to accept the possibility of Dave being in Blake's life was not something she was willing to hear. Instead of trying to get her to understand, I decided comfort was the best policy for now.

"I doubt that will be a concern of Dave's. A child would be a hinderance to his stardom. He's all about playing in clubs, not watching cartoons." I gave her hand a pat. "I doubt he will fight for much time."

Mom's furrowed brow didn't release. But she didn't push the subject further. Instead, she drank the last bit of her cooler and then sighed. "If you want to do this, I'll support it. I'll go to the meetings, and I'll sit in the courtroom. But I want you to know that we can figure this out on our own. We don't need him." Mom met my gaze, and I could feel her conviction.

That was all she wanted, an opportunity to take care of me. I doubted she'd ever thought I was going to come back. That's why she lost herself in that casino. And I couldn't fault her for that. After all, I was the queen of making wrong decisions.

"I know. This is only part A of my plan. Blake needs his father to chip in and help take care of him. I have other routes I want to try as well."

Mom quirked an eyebrow. "Really?"

I nodded and then yawned. Our conversation, mixed with the day-long trip back, had worn me out. I was fairly certain that I could sleep for days. I stretched my arms over my head. "But I'm beat and still have some things to work out. I'll let you know once they are in place."

The corner of Mom's lips tipped up as she studied me. For the first time in a long time, she looked hopeful. "I'm excited to hear this plan," she said.

Truth was, it was only a small plan. One that included me finding a job that I could bring my son to and that would pay me a lot of money. And I was fairly certain that a job like that didn't just appear because you wished for it hard enough.

But still, I was going to force myself to remain optimistic.

I was going to find the job that I needed in order to help my mother and take care of my son. And I was going to win the child support hearing as quickly and painlessly as possible with Dave being completely cordial.

I was going to use these positive affirmations until I manifested the reality I wanted.

Sure, it might be a bunch of mumbo jumbo, but I was going to do it. After all, what other choice did I have?

I was the master of my own destiny, and I was going to take control of it.

Starting tonight.

VICTORIA

It had been a week since Brett and I broke up, and it had been hell. It was as if Brett had already moved on. Every time I saw him, he was smiling and talking to guests at the inn or the other employees. Even with me, he seemed relaxed. He even joked with me—which only made me feel worse.

Either he'd moved on from me, which meant that I was easy to get over, or he was so hurt that he had to put up this fake front. I wasn't sure which option was better, so I decided the best thing for me to do was move forward and forget the week we'd spent together. The week where I'd allowed someone into my life more than I'd allowed anyone else before.

I walked into the kitchen Saturday morning and glanced around. Brett was nowhere to be found, so I dug through the drawer of aprons until I found one that would fit and strung it over my neck. I walked around the room as I tied the strings into a bow behind me.

Just as I passed by the office, I heard a voice that caused me to stop.

"Maggie, will you... Idiot."

I peeked around the door to find Archer hiding behind the desk. I had to step forward to see that he was down on one knee with a ring box clutched in his shaky hands. He looked physically ill as he knelt there.

"I'm thinking you don't want to say, 'Maggie will you idiot,' if you want her to say yes."

Archer sprang up, and his gaze whipped over to me. He looked panicked as he glanced behind me. He hastily shoved the ring box into his pocket and swiped his brow. "Is there anyone else in the kitchen?"

I took a few steps back and glanced into the empty room. I shook my head and moved to shut the door. At least focusing on his relationship with Maggie would help me forget my extremely painful, nonexistent one. "All clear," I said once the door latch engaged.

Archer collapsed on the desk chair and let out his breath. I gave him a supportive smile as I moved to sit on the small fraying chair in the corner. "You doing okay?" I asked.

Archer glanced over at me as he twisted in the chair. "Just panicking."

I chuckled. I could relate. Every relationship I'd ever been in always ended with me panicking in one shape or another. And the most recent relationship was the latest victim.

But I didn't understand why he was so worried. Archer and Maggie seemed so in sync. They were perfect for each other. Anyone with eyes could see that. So why was this step a hard one for him?

"Are you afraid Maggie will say no?" That couldn't be the reason. Maggie was head over heels in love with him. He had to know that.

Archer glanced up at me; his expression weakened. He shook his head as he dropped his focus to his hands. "That's not it. I know Maggie loves me, and I love her. But there's something stopping me. I don't know if my ex is in my head…" His voice drifted off to a whisper. "Or my daughter."

My chest squeezed at his words. I never had a chance to meet either, but I knew how loyal Archer was. Losing both had to be a major blow to him. "I'm sure your daughter just wants you to be happy. And your ex? She shouldn't be the reason you don't do this." I waved toward the pocket where he'd stashed the ring earlier.

Archer grew quiet for a moment before he sighed. "But why do I deserve to be happy? I had the perfect family life, and I lost it." He scrubbed his face with his hand. "Why do I get to be so lucky to have a do-over? I know I wasn't the best husband or the best father. I should have tried harder. Done more." Panic began to rise in his voice. I could tell that this was a conversation that he'd had multiple times with himself.

And I was the perfect person to recognize it because the same self-doubt talk was a daily occurrence in my own mind. But it was strange hearing it from someone who seemed so strong, so confident, and was in a loving relationship with a woman who adored him.

"Do you love Maggie?" When someone was spiraling, it was best to start with the basics. When they could focus on what they did know, it helped them deal with the things that they didn't.

Archer paused and then looked up at me. I could see the confidence in his gaze as he nodded. "More than anything in the world."

"Do you want to make her happy?"

He nodded again. "Every day."

"Do you promise to remain faithful to her? Love her like she deserves?"

He nodded again.

"Then you deserve to be happy as well." I leaned forward. "Do you trust her happiness with someone else?"

He frowned. "No."

"If you don't trust her happiness with someone else, and you want her to be happy, then I think you know what you need to do."

Archer paused before he shifted so he could pull the ring from his pocket. He flipped the box open and stared at the ring. "I'm going to propose."

I clapped my hands. "There you go. Use that confidence and go ask her."

Archer stood but then hesitated. I shook my head.

"Don't stop. Don't think. Just go ask her now. She doesn't want pomp and circumstance. She wants you, Archer. You and all your flaws."

Archer's shoulders squared as I spoke. I could see his determination as it settled in his features. He loved Maggie, and I had no doubt that they were going to have a wonderful life together.

Which only heightened my awareness that I was not going to have that wonderful life with someone I loved. And that left an ache in my chest that wouldn't go away anytime soon.

Archer moved to open the door but then paused. I geared myself up for another pep talk only to have him turn and face me head-on.

"I talked to Brett."

My stomach churned. What did that mean? "Oh, yeah?"

He nodded. "I think you may need to take some of the same medicine you are dishing out." After a withering gaze, he turned the handle and strode from the room.

Just as he cleared the doorway, Brett stepped into view. He watched Archer leave and then glanced in my direction. For the first time that week, I saw his mask slip, and the pain that I'd caused him floated to the surface.

But then that moment of vulnerability was gone, and he was back to *everything is fine*. "Every time I see you two, you're always behind a shut door." He frowned. "Should I be worried?"

I wanted to laugh at his joke. I wanted to pretend that I hadn't ruined everything between us. But I knew that was petty. That it didn't take into consideration how he was feeling. Asking him to forget my cruelty wasn't fair. In fact, the whole time we'd been spending together hadn't been fair to him at all.

He'd gone into our relationship with both eyes open. He was willing to take a leap into the deep end while I was over here guarding my heart like that was all that mattered. I'd led him on but then shut him out. And he deserved better.

But that didn't mean I couldn't be that better person for him.

Feeling confident yet scared, I stood up from the chair and crossed the room at a speed that I didn't know I could manage. Suddenly, I was standing in front of him. My heart was pounding, and my head was screaming for me to walk away, to avoid the thing that could cause me more pain than anything else.

Because if I opened myself up to Brett completely, he would see the good, the bad, and the ugly that resided underneath the surface of Victoria Holt. And what if that scared him off? What if I couldn't convince him that he wanted to stick around for that woman?

"Victoria?" Brett asked. His voice had deepened, and his gaze looked worried.

For the first time, I could see the real pain that I'd caused him.

Before I allowed myself to analyze what I was going to say, to calculate what was going to cause the least amount of damage to the facade I'd created for myself, I let my heart speak.

"I'm scared." My voice was barely a whisper, but I forced the words out as I held his gaze.

"You're scared of me?"

I shook my head. He wasn't the one that had me terrified. In fact, it was exactly the opposite. He was the sun shining in my darkened life. He made me feel happy and free.

He made me feel whole.

And I could lean on that until I found the happiness within myself.

"I'm scared of me. And what you'll do when you discover the person hiding underneath all of this."

He studied me for a moment as if he were chewing on my words. Then his hand slid down my arm until his fingers cupped mine, and he brought my hand up to press to his lips.

"I don't know what dark storms you have going on inside, but I want you to give me the chance to weather them." His lips brushed my hand once more before he glanced back up at me. "I'm stronger than I look, and I don't scare easily."

All of the pain. All of the uncertainty that I'd been holding inside of me for so long finally bubbled to the surface, and I couldn't hold back the tears that clung to my lids. They escaped and rolled down my cheeks.

"I'm broken," I whispered. If I was going to reveal everything, I might as well reveal everything right now. That way, if he was going to run, he would do it now.

He shrugged. "I'm great at fixing things." He brought my

hand to his shoulder and set it there. Then he moved his hand to my waist, pulling me closer to him.

"I'm stubborn."

He leaned in, kissing the tip of my nose. "I'm pretty convincing."

The butterflies that were rushing around my stomach were attesting to that statement.

"I'm scared."

He kissed my forehead and then moved to meet my gaze. "Me too." Then he brought his free hand up to my cheek, his thumb brushing my lips. "But there's no one I'd rather start this journey with than you."

I drew my eyebrows together as I studied him. Part of me was convinced that I was going to discover the lie. That he didn't mean the words he was saying.

"You're never going to find it," he whispered.

"What?"

"Whatever excuse you are trying to locate inside of my intentions. You're never going to find it." He chuckled. His laugh was soothing to my ears.

"I won't?"

He shook his head. "Nope. Because it's not there. I want to be with you because of who *you* are. That's it. Plain and simple."

A warmth exploded throughout my body at his words. He'd seen the worst of me, yet he still wanted to be around me. Despite the fact that I'd pushed him away, he refused to go.

For the first time, someone in my life wasn't dropping

me the first chance they got. Who I was inside meant more to them than the person I wasn't.

"Are you sure?"

Brett pulled away, so he could stare at me. His gaze was so open and so raw that it took my breath away. Then his lips were on mine as he pulled me close. It was as if he wanted me to feel how he felt about me. He wanted me to know that he was never going to let me go.

Soon, I found myself leaning into the kiss. Moving with his mouth as he moved against mine. I parted my lips and let him in. I could feel his passion for me, and I wanted to return the feeling. Because I felt it for this man.

Oh, how I felt it for this man.

Eventually, we pulled apart. The air around me felt heavy when I did. Brett's arms were still around my waist, but I was far enough away to be able to focus on his features.

"What do you say? Want a do-over?" he asked as he gently kissed the tip of my nose again.

I narrowed my eyes. "How many do I get?"

He laughed and pulled back. "How many do you need?"

I shrugged. "Well, cats have nine lives. So, nine?"

He grimaced. "You're going to put me through that eight more times?"

I pressed my hands against his chest and tried to push away. "If you don't think that Victoria Holt is going to need more do-overs, then maybe we should just end it here."

Brett tightened his grip on me and pulled me back. He

shook his head. "All right, fine. You can get eight more do-overs."

I settled into his arms, my hands resting on his chest. I could feel his heartbeat. It was strong and sturdy and exactly what I needed in my chaotic life.

Even though I was short-tempered and broken, Brett managed to see the good in me. He was willing to take me on with all of my craziness and even give me second chances.

I would be a fool to let him go.

And Victoria Holt was no fool.

I knew I had a good thing here, and I would spend the rest of my life letting him know that.

I was never going to let him go.

He was mine.

Forever.

19

FIONA

I stood in Clementine's studio surrounded by white streamers and white balloons. A giant cake sat in the middle of one of the folding tables with the word *Congrats* written in teal frosting. Little ring confetti littered the table around the cake, and a huge banner was hung up on the mirror wall that spelled out the same message.

Archer had proposed to Maggie, and she'd said yes. So, for our book club meeting, Clementine decided to forgo the usual—or should I say the new normal—meeting and throw a celebration. She invited half the town, which only made her tiny dance studio feel smaller.

Shari spotted me and weaved her way through the crowd. I gave her a weak smile, to which she chuckled and nodded. "I know. Clem went overboard, but that's kind of her thing."

I shrugged. "I guess she had poor Jake up all night blowing up these balloons."

"I can see that."

"She's a dork."

"But we love her."

I nodded. Silence engulfed us. I could tell that Shari wanted to ask me about my meeting with her brother-in-law, but I wasn't quite ready to talk about it. Dave was digging in his heels, which meant mediation wasn't going to work for us.

We were going to have to go to court. It wasn't what I wanted, but with how Dave was acting, I was ready to fight this. Blake deserved it.

Before we could talk further, Clem shouted for everyone to be quiet because Maggie was here. We crouched behind each other, but there was nowhere to hide. It was literally just a room with four walls.

As soon as the door opened, we all shouted, "Surprise!"

Maggie screamed and clutched her chest. Once she realized what was happening, she laughed and began hugging everyone.

The party picked up, and soon, my problems with Dave moved to the back burner. I was going to celebrate my best friend and her happiness.

Just as the party began to wane and people began to leave, the studio door opened, and a hush fell over the crowd. I glanced up, stretching to the side to see who had walked in. It wasn't until Maggie said, "Penny?" that I realized Maggie's mom was standing in the middle of the crowd who had parted to let her through.

"What are you doing here?" Maggie asked.

Penny glanced around before she parted her lips and said, "I'm moving to Magnolia for the next few months."

There were audible gasps around the room. We weren't in the dark about Maggie and Penny's relationship. I glanced over at Maggie to gauge her reaction. She looked surprised as she studied her mom.

Then she smiled and gave her a hug. "Well, then, welcome. We're excited to have you stay."

***

I hope you enjoyed Magnolia at Midnight. I loved diving into Victoria's romance and discovering Fiona's inner strength.

I can't wait for A Magnolia Wedding where Maggie gets her happily ever after even if Penny is moving to Magnolia. Plus, I have a recluse author planned for Fiona's hero. It's going to be amazing!

Grab you copy HERE!

Want more Red Stiletto Bookclub Romances?? Head on over and grab you next read HERE.

For a full reading order of Anne-Marie's books, you can find them HERE.

Or scan below:

Printed in Great Britain
by Amazon